SACRED LOVE

Sam was just about to grab her by the arm to pull her back when he noticed Fred's clothing and shoes, as if they were set out fresh that very morning over the back of a dark leather chair. It was unusual, but Sam felt his skin prickle with misgiving. Bailey's gasp at the bathroom door did not surprise him.

"Sam! He's . . . dead."

His heart heavy, Sam joined Bailey at the open door of the huge bathroom. It was true. Fred Durham lay in a tub of bathwater, probably dead by electrocution. In his lap was a handheld blow-dryer.

In shock, Bailey lost the ability to move or breathe. She was rooted to the rug on the bathroom floor, her eyes wide and her mouth hanging open.

Sam took charge of his wife and of the moment. There was nothing anyone could do for Fred now. "Let's alert the others and then call the police."

As Bailey leaned on him, Sam led her away from the bathroom, out the bedroom door, and down the stairs to the first floor. Through the windows of the Painted Lady, the fog was thick as ever, its presence ominous.

SACRED LOVE

SHELBY LEWIS

ARABESQUE
★ BET
BOOKS

BET Publications, LLC
www.bet.com
www.arabesquebooks.com

ARABESQUE BOOKS are published by

BET Publications, LLC
c/o BET BOOKS
One BET Plaza
1900 W Place NE
Washington, D.C. 20018-1211

All Kensington Titles, Imprints, and Distributed Lines are available at special quantity discounts for bulk purchases for sales promotions, premiums, fund-raising, and educational or institutional use. Special book excerpts or customized printings can also be created to fit specific needs. For details, write or phone the office of the Kensington special sales manager: Kensington Publishing Corp., 850 Third Avenue, New York, NY 10022, attn: Special Sales Department, Phone: 1-800-221-2647.

BET Books is a trademark of Black Entertainment Television, Inc. ARABESQUE, the ARABESQUE logo, and the BET BOOKS logo are trademarks and registered trademarks.

First Printing: August 2001
10 9 8 7 6 5 4 3 2 1

Printed in the United States of America

For Kendra Gabrielle

Crime is terribly revealing. Try and vary your methods as you will your tastes, your habits, your attitude of mind, and your soul is revealed by your actions.

—Hercule Poirot
The A.B.C. Murders by Agatha Christie

A Succulent Supper for Two

Baked Salmon

Parmesan Rice

Green Salad

Apricot Pound Cake

Raspberry Mint Coolers

who flicked a casual look in Grant's direction.

ONE

It was the first week of June. Bailey Walker hummed while she worked in her large country kitchen. A part-time caterer, she enjoyed those times when she made food for her own family, a welcome respite from the busy work schedule she maintained before the summer season, her least busy time of the calendar year.

During the summer, when outdoor barbecues outnumbered indoor sit-down dinners, Bailey preferred to relax with her husband, Sam, and their two daughters, Fern and Sage. On this summer evening, she prepared a romantic dinner for herself and Sam.

Bailey brushed the fresh salmon on each side with melted butter. She sprinkled just enough salt and pepper on the filets to bring out the distinctive flavor of the food. After placing the fish in a shallow glass baking dish, its surface liberally coated with butter, she slid the dish in the oven, set at 350 degrees, for thirty minutes. When the fish was done, it would flake on the fork and melt in the mouth. Salmon was one of Sam's favorite foods.

To make the parmesan rice, she placed the grains in a pot of cold water, which she brought to a boil.

Bailey put the lid on the pot and turned the heat to low. After the rice steamed, she added butter, parmesan cheese, fresh cream, egg yolks, chopped parsley, seasoned salt, and pepper. She placed the mixture in a casserole dish, its bottom lightly buttered, and baked it in the oven once the salmon had cooked.

The green salad was a cinch to make, especially when the greens came straight from Bailey's kitchen garden, which she kept in a small fenced area outside her back door. She used romaine lettuce, Boston lettuce, and watercress. After carefully washing and drying the greens, she ripped them into small pieces. She added cucumber, red onion, mushrooms, and chives to the greens. The French dressing was homemade.

While the salad chilled in the refrigerator, Bailey prepared the batter for the apricot pound cake, her own special favorite. She creamed the butter and sugar together. To this she added six eggs, one at a time. She sifted together the flour, salt, and baking powder. Once this was done, she alternated the dry ingredients with sour cream. To the batter she added apricot nectar, and lemon, orange, and almond extract. She poured the batter into a Bundt pan and baked the cake for an hour and ten minutes at 350 degrees. Before the cake cooled completely on a wire rack, Bailey punched holes in the top with a toothpick and drizzled a mixture of fresh-squeezed lemon and confectioners' powdered sugar on top.

The beverage was easy to make. She boiled raspberry jam, fresh mint, and water. After an hour, she strained the juice, added squeezed lemon and cold carbonated water. The drink would be perfect over cubed ice.

Bailey set the dining room table for two. She used her everyday creamware dishes, but dressed the table with David Austin roses, fronds of asparagus fern, and half a dozen white votive candles, which she set between the fragrant roses and delicate ferns.

In the background, she listened to Brandy's compact disc, *Never Say Never,* and the song "Almost Doesn't Count." She enjoyed the entire collection of songs and sang them, off-key, while she righted her kitchen prior to Sam's arrival home for dinner. She did not make a huge meal every day, but today was special. She had received an invitation from her favorite uncle, Fred Durham.

It was the middle of June, and underneath the quiet domestic scene, Bailey was restless. After the dishes were washed and the counters returned to order, she sat at the nook table and listened to the next song on Brandy's compact disc, "Top of the World," and knew she was anything but; she was happy with her life in general, yet itching for something to do other than tending to her husband, her children, and her catering career. Bailey wanted an adventure.

She studied the slim envelope she held in her hand. The stationery, expensive cream vellum, was inscribed with a heavy black scrawl, the sight of which thrilled her. Home alone, in a house too quiet for her liking, Bailey wanted nothing more than to get out of New Hope, California, even if she only left for a brief weekend. What she needed was different air, fresh experience, one-on-one with her husband.

She and Sam had married in June, the third weekend in the month, but over the years, after the arrival of their children, and after the onset of financial responsibilities, they had grown out of the habit of taking a weekend trip to celebrate the anniversary of their marriage; once again, for this year, they had no getaway planned.

Instead of stepping away from their everyday lives, they settled on dinner and small gifts to mark their exclusive holiday. This ritual started out as a way to save money in the early years of their marriage, done for convenience during the latter. Bailey wanted to break that habit, and the invitation she held in her hand was a perfect opportunity to do that very thing.

Bailey had not seen Uncle Fred in a year. At eighty-seven, he traveled one of the seven continents during the first six months of the calendar year, the United States during the last six months of the calendar year. His travels made his conversation highly entertaining.

On those occasions when Fred Durham resided at his northern California mansion, located in a prestigious section of San Francisco, he often invited one of his many relatives, close or distant, to join him at his hillside home, a Victorian structure he called, affectionately, his Painted Lady.

The Painted Lady, a turquoise building with mauve trim and dark purple-colored doorways, was three stories tall, and nearly four thousand square feet in living space. There were servants' quarters, two kitchens, a formal dining room, one parlor, a study, a library, six bedrooms, six baths, and three fireplaces.

Bailey itched to see the Painted Lady again. She referred to the house, like everyone else in the Durham family, as if the building truly lived—Uncle Fred would have it no other way, one of his many idiosyncrasies.

A bachelor by choice, eccentric by design, Fred Durham had made his fortune designing elaborate, one-of-a-kind carriages in the Victorian era tradition. Each carriage was handcrafted, built of fine materials, and guaranteed to last a lifetime, seventy-five years. They were also ridiculously expensive.

Quaint, historical towns across the United States used Durham Carriages to cart tourists through historic districts, such as Nob Hill and Russian Hill, two San Francisco neighborhoods embellished with Baroque mansions, most of them custom built by the silver tycoons of the 1860s.

Fred's paternal grandfather, John Durham, had made his first fortune in silver. An escaped Georgia slave, John hired himself as a cook for a cattle outfit moving longhorns from Texas to Wyoming. From Wyoming, John made his way farther West, eventually striking it rich in a Nevada silver mine; he became an instant tycoon.

Money in hand, John erected a saloon in San Francisco, a profitable bar he called Sweet Revenge. Sweet Revenge generated enough income for John to build a house on Dark Hill, a neighborhood largely comprising black merchants and office professionals.

In the 1960s, about the time Rosa Parks created a local, then national scandal by refusing to take a back seat on a public bus in Alabama, Fred inherited the house on Dark Hill, his Painted Lady, and for the next forty years, the house proved to be his lifetime obsession.

It was Fred who carefully restored the declining Victorian, floor by floor, until the house thrived as a beautiful masterpiece. By annual invitation, he

encouraged select members of the Durham family
to spend time with him and his lady.

For Fred, it was the house on Dark Hill that best
represented his life's pride, his life's joy, far more
than the lucrative carriage business ever could. By
sending the heavy cream vellum invitation to
Bailey, he wished to share this joy with her; she
could not wait to tell Sam.

Bailey studied the embossed invitation, a curve
on her lips. By the 1980s, an invitation to Uncle
Fred's mansion had become a coveted treat within
the Durham family, worth its weight in Nevada-
mined silver. Bailey's father, Uncle Fred's nephew,
was a Durham, and she was his oldest child. She
felt obligated to accept the invitation, especially
now that her father was no longer alive.

In June, the hundred-year-old Victorian mansion
was as likely to begin its day enshrouded with fog
as it was to end its day the same way. The San
Francisco Bay inspired the fog, which in turn
added to the mystique of Dark Hill.

There were those who said the Hill was haunted
with the souls of tycoons who lost their fortunes
in the gambling saloons of the 1800s, in the stock
markets of the 1900s, and the Internet gambling
of the twenty-first century.

It was also on the Internet that new multimillionaires made their marks, entrepreneurial mavens
who dropped out of college to start businesses that
flourished from home office computers.

It was the new multimillionaires who orches-
trated the rebirth of Dark Hill, a community re-
vival that Bailey knew delighted her uncle. Now
the largest portion of homes in the legendary
neighborhood looked as good as his own Painted
Lady. No longer was his home a stunning jewel

set on old, expensive velvet, slowly falling apart at the seams.

To this day, Dark Hill remained mostly black, but had diversified with citizens from around the world: East Indians, Hispanics, Africans, Arabs, Asians, and Russians flocked to the area in ever-increasing numbers, particularly to the loft apartments in those mansions that had been converted from single-dwelling homes into multiple units.

These were people drawn to the unique neighborhood because of its close proximity to the ornate masonry of downtown skyscrapers, the fabulous waterfront retail shops, the scrumptious seafood, the fingertip commerce, domestic and international, the twenty-four-hour entertainment, the one-of-a-kind mansions, some Edwardian, most Victorian, all crammed together on near-zero lots.

If it was true that tourists lost their hearts in San Francisco, Bailey understood why: The bustling city was sensational. She loved San Francisco, its fabled cable cars, skinny alleys, and steep hills, its history of twin extremes: ridiculous riches and pitiful poverty. Most important, she loved her Uncle Fred. A getaway weekend with her husband to the Painted Lady, Bailey decided, was the perfect anecdote to her restless state.

The sound of a key opening the front door signaled Sam's arrival. It was Friday evening, and she knew he would be tired. Drawn by the smell of delicious food, he entered the kitchen, its ambience set to soothe, its hostess anxious to share the fruit of her labor.

The vice president of electronic engineering in a prominent computer chip manufacturing firm, Sam savored his daily arrival into Bailey's kitchen, especially after a rough business day like the one he had just left behind, a day wrought with computer system failures, exacerbated by political infighting between upper management and its staff, his staff.

The scent of baked salmon on a warm June night was both unexpected and welcome. He placed his keys and briefcase on the kitchen counter, took one look at the delight on Bailey's face, and braced himself for a surprise. "What's up?"

She laughed, then gave him a quick kiss on the lips. His skin felt warm, comfortingly familiar. "You know me too well."

He scanned her attire, relaxed-fit jeans, open-toed sandals, and red tank top. Her hair, smooth and bobbed, shined beneath the soft ceiling lights. She exuded health and vitality, just what he needed to revive his senses. "It's been twenty years. I guess that makes you my best friend."

She eyed her husband with quick familiarity. He was thicker in the middle than he had been when they first met, yet he remained built like the athlete he was. Sam ran five miles a day, every morning, before going to work. "I can't believe how time has flown."

"What's that in your hand?"

"An invitation from Uncle Fred."

Sam smiled. "He must be ninety now."

"Eighty-seven."

"Is this one of his infamous summonses?"

"Of course," said Bailey.

Sam's smile was gone now, in its place, a searching look. When he spoke, his tone was neutral. "And of course you want to go."

"I figured we could both use a break."

Sam lifted the stationery from Bailey's open

palm. He read the brief note silently, his face without expression. "Three weeks from now? It will be our anniversary."

"We could visit Uncle Fred, do some sight-seeing," Bailey said.

Sam thought of the many things he had to do at the office, studied the anticipation on his wife's face, and expelled a long breath. "Let's do it."

She was relieved. Over the years, his responsibility had increased to the point that he was on-call day and night to troubleshoot production problems. Many of his accounts brought millions of dollars to his employer, and it was Sam's job to make sure production ran as smooth as possible, even if it meant handling middle of the night phone calls about problems that might cut efficiency or hurt company sales. Those late nights away from home were rough on their relationship.

"I thought you might say that," Bailey said. "Thanks, Sam."

He kissed her forehead. "No problem."

"I'll ask your parents to keep the girls."

"They'd be offended if we didn't."

"Fern and Sage are spoiled out of their minds," said Bailey, her tone half amused, half disgusted.

"And I wouldn't have them any other way," he said.

"Me either," said Bailey as she set platters of food on the table for them to share. "To tell you the truth, Sam, the girls are the best thing I've ever done." She spoke wistfully, her fingers deft as she perfected the table setting.

Sam wished he had brought home candy for her or lingerie, a special gift that showed his appreciation of the large and small ways she eased his passage through life. When had he stopped bringing her jewelry out of the blue? It was not enough to provide food, clothing, shelter, and to pay the bills. Those were the basics of being a good husband, like courtesy and fidelity.

The basics were expected, but the romance, that sweet song of desire and oneness between lovers, had to be protected with effort, the way silver is protected from the tarnish of time, the abuse of constant handling.

Bailey was Sam's grand passion, but when had he last expressed his great love for her beyond the privacy of their bedroom, beyond the rose- and candle-laden dinner table now set for two? It had been a long time since he last courted his wife, too long, and for one grave moment, Sam felt shame. Lately, he had been more absorbed in maintaining his company's production lines than his marriage vows: to love, honor, and cherish his bride.

Sam loved his wife, he honored her, but he had fallen down on the cherishing part by not spoiling her with the gift of time—time spent in conversation designed for her ears alone, time spent in malls or boutiques selecting gifts she alone would treasure.

He was the only man authorized to buy her silk and satin, things she loved to wear next to her skin, things he loved to see her wear, yet he saved the gift-buying tasks for some other day, a day that rarely came now that so much of his energy went into his job.

It was a wonder Bailey still made time to please him, when he made so little time for her. He spoke from the heart. "The best thing I ever did was marry you."

She heard him, detected the regret in his tone,

and felt a surge of anger. At the kitchen sink, she stared out the window at her garden. The yard was decorated with flowers and vegetables she tended as well as she cared for her husband and children. Whatever Bailey touched seemed to flourish, as if there was magic in her hands, a brand of power derived of faith, commitment, and a pleasure that ran deeper than mere food for the soul.

Yet, there she was, feeling anger at Sam's words, an odd stirring that was not soothed by the cultivated beauty of her David Austin roses and the peace of her well furnished, French-vanilla-scented home. She had reached the point in her life where the house no longer needed anything new, her child-rearing days would soon be over, her marriage almost two decades old, her husband's career and her own in full swing.

Her closet was stuffed with clothes, the car she drove was new. She was well established, firmly middle class and proud of it. Right then, with her husband gazing at her, expectation stamped on his handsome face, Bailey realized she knew all the secrets in her garden, that rich and fruitful place she called home.

For Bailey, no secrets meant no adventure. No adventure meant boredom. Boredom led to disorder: subversive behavior, sullen attitude, extreme discontent, each a form of misconduct rooted in anger. Bailey had learned there was no happily ever after in her marriage. There was happy, sad, and at this time in her life, an insidious sense of melancholy.

This downward emotional trend had to be stopped, she reasoned, and the first step to a brighter marital mood was open conversation.

"We've been together for so long," Bailey said. "Don't you get tired?"

"Forgetful is more like it," Sam said.

Her gaze left the garden beyond the kitchen window to study him. Dressed in a white chambray shirt, navy slacks with matching shoes, he managed to look sexy and professional. His muscles were thick but strong, contoured instead of flabby. With or without clothes, Sam had whip appeal.

Her tone was guarded. "What do you mean?"

His eyes, dark and watchful, tried to assess her mood. The table was set for two, but romance was not in the air. "I get so caught up in work and entertaining business colleagues and traveling for the company that I forget what's really important."

"Family," Bailey said. She stopped looking at him. Businesslike, she put the cooled cake on a pedestal platter, a vintage dish made of pale peach crystal. She decorated the outer edges of the cake with curled slices of lemon peel that she had rolled in white sugar.

He watched her every move and understood that what she needed to hear was honesty. He wished again for a box of her favorite chocolates, even a Hallmark card that said I love you.

"No, Bailey," Sam said. "You. I forget to take time out for you."

"We've been busy," Bailey said. "Two kids, two murder mysteries, thriving lives." She sighed, the sound heavy in the too-quiet room, the Brandy compact disc no longer in play. "We have a lot to be thankful for, Sam."

He took a step toward her, but refrained from touching her, from pulling her into his arms the way he wanted to just then, a gesture he sensed she would not appreciate. Right now, she wanted his complete attention, his mind totally in tune with hers. To be in tune, they needed understanding. Understanding meant communication.

Sam used his voice, smooth and deep, to express his sentiment. "All that's wonderful, Bailey, but without you, everything we have means nothing."

"You're forgetting the girls," Bailey said. "Nothing is more important than our children." As soon as the words were spoken, Bailey wondered at the truth in them. She had allowed her children, the raising of them, to fill so much of her time she worried about what she would do when her daughters left home and the nest she had built for them was no longer needed.

Bailey doubted she would want to cater full-time, and by then, Sam would probably be president of a company, a career transition that would push him further away from home, the demands on his time greater than ever before. He worked in a field where age and expertise added to his desirability. When their children were gone, he would still be fully occupied with his life's work.

He might find it easier to get along without the girls than she would. Still, how could he say that, without her, his world would be nothing? It was because of their children that they had developed the discipline to establish themselves in a solid neighborhood with solid schools and solid community values.

Witnessing her distress, Sam tried to explain. "In the last few years, we've been so hung up on raising the girls and 'making it' that we've lost sight of ourselves. You and me. Our home and our careers and our parenting have a time and a place and that doesn't mean forever. You and me. That's forever."

She visibly relaxed. "Damn, you're good."

He laughed, relieved her anger was a thing of the past. This time when he stepped forward, he pulled her into his arms, his chin resting against her forehead as she leaned into him. She felt familiar and right. He spoke softly. "What else is for dinner?"

"Me."

The look on his face was cocky, his stance as well. Eyebrows wiggling, he shucked his tie. "No need to tell me twice."

Bailey rushed to clarify. "*After* we have dinner and *after* I call Uncle Fred."

He laughed outright. In spite of the flowers and candles, she took their relationship for granted as much as he did. "How very practical, I mean, passionate of you."

"Very funny."

He tossed his tie in the direction of his briefcase. It slid across the battered black surface and landed on the counter. "I'm serious, Bailey. I remember a time when we were too starved for each other to even say the word *dinner*, let alone eat anything."

Suddenly she wished she had worn a pretty sundress instead of faded jeans, blazing red lipstick instead of serviceable bronze, her dark brown hair up with seductive wisps of curls framing her face instead of a sleek style.

Was it enough to make his favorite dinner, to set a romantic mood for two, only to sabotage the moment with talk of the way things used to be? She thought of the song "Happy," on the Brandy compact disc. Bailey was not exactly happy, but she did feel content. The difference was subtle, yet noteworthy. What happened when she no longer felt . . . content? "That was B.C.," she said.

"What?"

"Before children," she clarified.

He began to unbutton his shirt. He wore a tank-styled T-shirt underneath, the wiry hairs on his chest visible above the neckline. "Are we that bad?"

"I think so. After the last murder we solved, I think we were both so determined to be normal, that we switched from being adventurous to being the king and queen of the mundane."

"True."

She faced him squarely, aware that on the table, their food was slowly growing cold, aware that even after all the time spent preparing the meal, she really did not care: Food could be replaced, their relationship could not. She spoke from the heart, her voice a little wistful, a little sad. "We need to get reacquainted, Sam."

He watched her from hooded eyes, his head angled to one side as if measuring her melancholy. He should have noticed she had stopped suggesting places for them to go alone. Was it because, again, he had been immersed in his work to the point she stopped opening herself to the rejection of his many refusals? What was he working for if not for her happiness as well as his own? "I gather a weekend won't do it?"

"No," Bailey said, "but it's a start."

She sounded so sad, and suddenly, Sam had no desire for his wife to settle. He had not expected to see her running around the room in joy, not after twenty years of oneness, but he wished to at least see her glow. Her spirit was what concerned him, her spirit had lost its shine, like the diamond on a wedding ring, covered in a thin film of grime.

For Bailey, today was another day. Something in Sam rebelled against that resignation, a feeling so exquisite that it lay almost hidden beneath her general air of content. Perhaps they had been too careful, when in truth, happiness in life was never guaranteed.

The murders they helped solve in the past had shown them at least that much. Right now, with food growing cold on the table and candles burned a quarter of the way down, Sam realized how much he was missing by playing it safe; for one thing, he missed the glitter in Bailey's eyes. He wanted to see sparks in them again.

"How about this," Sam said. "How about we spend a weekend with Fred? After that, we tour the coastal towns down Highway One. We can start with Sausalito because it's closest to Fred's place in San Francisco and then make our way to the beaches in Santa Cruz and Carmel."

Bailey looked down at her hands. They were strong, capable hands, her only jewelry her wedding rings. "How much time are you talking here?"

"Fourteen days. Two full weeks."

Fourteen days. "We've never been away from the girls that long."

He understood her indecision. If he was gung ho about climbing the corporate ladder, she was equally dedicated to the success of their home. On the positive side, their obsessions brought them accolades from family and friends, and on the negative side, their obsessions had proven detrimental to their love life.

"The girls aren't little anymore, Bailey," Sam

said. "Fern drives. Sage is a clone of my mother. Fern will probably drive those two to every mall between here and Daly City. Dad will get a break from Mom, since historically, he's been the shop-till-you-drop chauffeur. It won't hurt the girls to have a vacation from us, either. Besides, my parents will love it."

Bailey's smile was brief, edged with satisfaction. "We've really been lucky in that department."

"You call Fred," Sam said. "I'll call Mom and Dad."

"I wish my parents were still alive," Bailey said, even though she loved her in-laws very much. "If Sage is like your mom, Fern is just like mine. My mother was practical and very take-charge."

A look of consternation crossed Sam's face. "Where are the girls anyway?" Normally, they were in the kitchen prowling inside the refrigerator or the cookie jar for snacks. He was so caught up in his conversation with Bailey, he never noticed the girls were missing.

"At the mall. Where else?"

Sam laughed. "While you're calling Fred, I'll wash up."

Bailey dialed her uncle's phone number, then wedged the portable phone between her shoulder and ear while she set the salad on the table. After six rings, Fred answered himself. She teased him. "What? No maid? No butler to answer the phone?"

Fred's voice boomed across the telephone line. "Is this Bailey?"

"It is."

"You sound like your mother."

Bailey's smile was there in her tone. "Thanks."

"Does this call mean you're coming to see me?"

Hard of hearing, Fred habitually talked louder

than necessary. Bailey held the phone away from her ear, which did little to lessen the power of Fred's voice. He was definitely excited about her call. She said, "How could I resist?"

He was quick to quip. "You can't."

"You're a mess, Uncle Fred."

"What I am is old, Bailey." After a slight pause, he said a bit slyly, "I've got something I want to give you."

Fred lowered his voice to the point where she had to press the phone to her ear, which was highly unusual, and for one disconcerting moment, very suspicious to Bailey. In response to his shift in attitude, Bailey found herself automatically adjusting the tone of her own voice, so that she, too, spoke more softly.

She had not spoken this soft to Fred in years. Because he heard her, she figured he wore a newer, more efficient hearing aid than the one he had the last time she saw him. "You don't need to give me anything," she said. "I'm just thankful for the invitation. As soon as I saw that trademark D of yours on the envelope, I was thrilled. I can't wait to see you."

Another pause, this one a little longer than the other. "Sam coming?"

"Of course," Bailey said. Sam had returned to the kitchen in jeans and a short-sleeved Polo shirt, its hunter green color complimenting his skin. With his head, he motioned for her to hang up the phone and join him at the dinner table. He was ravenous.

"Good," Fred said. He was back to shouting.

Bailey's frown expressed her concern about his odd behavior, from shouting to low speaking to shouting again. Even though her uncle could not see her face, Sam could. He mouthed, "Everything okay?"

She shrugged in response, as if to say, "How should I know?" Instead, she asked Fred, "Is there something wrong?"

He never missed a beat. "Just some little oddities here and there, mostly old age. My brain works perfectly. It's the rest of me that's falling apart."

He used a teasing, lighthearted tone, but she was not convinced everything was all right. "Aren't you well?"

"Overall, yes."

Bailey pondered the word *overall* for a moment. Coming from Fred, it was an interesting choice. The word stuck out because her uncle was not an in-between kind of person; he was either sick or not sick, happy or mad. "You've always been steady as the Golden Gate Bridge," she said.

"Aah, but the bridge sways, my darling."

"True, and it still stands."

His laugh, brief as it was, held a trace of irony. "Touché."

Bailey, always nosy, could not resist asking one more time. After all, he was her favorite uncle, and she loved him. If he had a problem, he might feel better discussing it with someone who truly cared about him on a personal level, a rare thing in his line of business.

Fred had once told Bailey that he second-guessed the motives of every new person who approached him about a personal relationship; he never knew who wanted Fred the man or Fred the millionaire. She would not see him for another three weeks, a very long time if trouble was brewing. "Then, what's up?"

"You'll have to wait until you get here. There's—"
His pause drove Bailey crazy. "—much to discuss."

"You've got me in suspense, Uncle Fred." She
wished she could see his face, get a true feel for
what he was up to with his handwritten invitation
and his curious conversation.

He smacked a kiss. "Until we meet again, my
sweet."

She laughed. "You're a mess."

"And you, my dear, are worth more than a million."

TWO

Thursday, Three Weeks Later

Sybil Durham's mouth dropped open the minute Sam entered the parlor at the Painted Lady. He wore dark navy slacks with a beige crew-collar shirt. He was clean shaven, his attitude vital and friendly. She said the first brazen thought on her mind. "Hey, got any brothers?"

"Two," Sam said. When he agreed to visit Fred with Bailey, he had forgotten he might run into Bailey's blunt, eccentric relatives. His wife was not the only member of the Durham clan who was nosy—the trait ran in the family.

"Two," Sybil said, a calculated gleam in her eyes.

"Both my brothers are married." This was said with more than a little bit of satisfaction. Sam had never liked Sybil. Dark skinned, cover-model chic, adorned in heavy costume jewelry, she was the kind of woman who hit on every powerhouse man who entered a room, single, married, young, or old. A connoisseur of male flesh, Sybil Durham wore men on her arm the way she wore her jewelry, boldly, with plenty of pizzazz.

She had been married five times and was currently without a husband. There was no way Sam

would recommend anyone he knew to her as a
potential dating prospect. As far as he was concerned, Sybil was a man-eater, the female version
of a womanizer; she lured a man with her beauty,
charmed her way into his circle of influential
friends, then picked his financial bones clean before moving on to the next conquest. As far as
Sam could tell, Sybil had little conscience to spare.

Bailey tucked her arm in her husband's, his taut
muscles a reflection of the strain he felt at Sybil's
words. Bailey could not believe the nerve of her
cousin. Ten years apart in age, she and Sybil had
never run in the same social or private circles. The
Durham bloodline was thin between them, and at
the moment, that line was nearly transparent.

"Get a life," Bailey said.

Sybil's laugh was sensual and throaty. She knew
precisely where she stood in Bailey's eyes, an animosity that was mutual. Sybil hated Bailey's apple-
pie image almost as much she hated being without
her own man during an evening destined to drive
her to drink.

"That's what I'm trying to do, little cousin," Sybil said. "It just occurred to me how much I
might've missed by not getting to know your husband's side of the family. I've never taken the time
to be that . . . friendly."

"Don't bother starting now," Bailey said. She
looked elegant and proud in a burgundy lace
sheath, the hem of her dress cut just above the
knees. Together, she and Sam made a striking pair.
"What are you doing here anyway?"

"Dear Uncle Fred invited me and the rest of the
family for dinner tonight." Sybil's smile was
crooked. "I see he's up to his usual tricks. I gather
you and Hunk Delicious over there didn't know

you'd be sharing the house with the gang all here."

"It's true," Bailey said, "I hadn't realized you all were coming."

Sybil was quick to pick up the subtle resentment in her cousin's voice. She gave in to the urge to needle Bailey. "Would it have changed your mind?"

"It might have."

"Then maybe that's why dear Uncle Fred didn't tell you."

Bailey had come to the Painted Lady to relax, but if her cousin wanted a fight, she would get one tonight. Bailey could barely keep a sneer out of her voice. "You are so sarcastic, so typical. I'm tired of your mouth already."

Sybil let her top lip curl in disgust. "As if I care what you think."

Before Bailey could make a scorching comeback, her uncle entered the emotion-charged parlor. He reminded her of a ballroom dancer: fluid and strong at the same time.

If he was truly ill, his grand entrance was well choreographed. Fred shouted his greeting. "Bailey! Sam!" To Sybil, he merely nodded, while his gaze, sharp, penetrating, remained on the Walkers.

To Bailey, her uncle did indeed look and behave physically fit, for which she was thankful. Although Fred was advanced in age, she could scarcely imagine life without him, even though his presence was largely at the perimeter of the world she had built with Sam, a world that centered on the two of them and their daughters.

In Bailey's mind, extended family usually meant Sam's relatives. It was Sam's mother who set the standard for the way she raised and tended her own family, Sam's brothers who would kick in with love and support should anything bad happen to Sam.

It was Sam's father who was the key to the entire Walker family, the man who laid the precedent of spending his bonus time with his family instead of spending that time on the job just to earn a few extra dollars. Sam's father valued sound family ties over dollar bills, a value system that was completely opposite the Durham family tradition, which placed moneymaking above family.

Sam's father's values anchored his family in a way that money never could, and those values were rooted in Sam. As Bailey searched the faces in her uncle's parlor, she calmed herself by tapping into her husband's solid root system, his stillness, his strength. Sam had never let her down.

Bolstered by her husband's quiet kind of love, Bailey ignored her cousin to focus on her uncle. Fred Durham was one of those vibrant people who filled a room with positive energy. Bailey matched that energy in a hug that warmed them both. The words she spoke were sincere. "It's good to see you."

Sam extended his hand to Fred, who pumped his palm in short, hard strokes. Fred and Bailey had the same smile, the same open attitude. Sam's response to Fred's smile of welcome was genuine. "Thanks for inviting us."

Fred stood between Sam and Bailey, an arm wrapped around each of them. The pressure he exerted to embrace them felt strong. He carried himself like a man who had just won big at poker. He spoke with relish. "The pleasure is all mine."

Sybil clapped her hands, slowly. "How incredibly touching." She sashayed to the wet bar, poured herself a short glass of bourbon, a vintage Spanish blend. "Really."

Fred eyed Sybil with thinly veiled skepticism. "You're just upset because your boy toy, Enrique, couldn't make it tonight. Or is it Carlos?" Fred frowned as if struggling hard to think. "Maurice? Tyrone?"

Sybil never spared him a glance. She downed her bourbon, then reached for the high-dollar bottle to pour herself another shot. She chose not to bother with ice, soda, or water. "You are just too cute, aren't you?"

At last, she shifted her glance from her drink preparations to stare at Fred. It was clear to Sam and Bailey she wanted to toss her drink in Fred's face, which she might have done had he been a man other than her aging rich uncle. Sybil did have boundaries, few, but specific.

Fred had too much money for her to risk truly getting on his bad side. She needed a loan, something she planned to hit him up for later that evening. All she needed was a private moment alone with him, ten minutes tops.

The sound of feet, a mixture of tapping and thudding, on the foyer floor captured everyone's attention. The moving feet belonged to Phoebe, Dexter, Tyra, and Grant, all Bailey's cousins, all wearing looks of curiosity in its various stages: inquisitive, meddling, anxious . . . odd.

Much to Bailey's surprise, the first and second cousins were not filing into the parlor in the midst of an argument, which was unusual; none of them got along particularly well. Watching them, Bailey was reminded of the Michael J. Fox movie in which Kirk Douglass played an elderly man whose immediate relatives were in a hurry for him to die in order for them to collect their inheritance.

Like the relatives in the movie, the Durhams were equally eccentric, equally needy, and just as ready for Fred to die. Bailey felt shame at their open avarice. She edged closer to Sam, her source of strength in the midst of her cousins' hard-fisted greed.

For a few uncomfortable moments, the assembled Durham kin meandered about the parlor, small talk cut to a minimum, suspicions primed high and set to blow at the first inopportune word.

Despite the blood ties, this was not a gathering of old friends. It was more like a stage, where every person in the parlor was involved in the portrayal of a tragedy that had yet to unfold. If greed were a demon, then its malignant spirit was fed by Bailey's cousins in the form of their eagerness, their desperation, their lust.

Sam spied Bailey's relatives as if they were as mysterious as the pyramids: He could see them, touch them, but the manner of their construction baffled his mind; that a family this dysfunctional belonged to Bailey astounded him.

For the first time, he understood an underlying part of his wife's character, why she devoted herself almost to obsession with the care of her family: It was the only family she truly had, the primary reason she cultivated and nurtured it. Sam's success as a man, at home and on the job, stemmed largely from the security her devotion provided him.

Because of Bailey, Sam went to work without worrying about his daughters, their safety, their education, or their foundation. He never worried that his home was out of order, that the money he earned was ever wasted, or that the love they shared was taken for granted.

In Bailey, Sam had found his soul mate, and for this, he was grateful to the Durham family. Without them, he would never have found the woman of his dreams. She deserved to be happy, and his response to the shenanigans of her family was important to her, his response could make or break her homecoming.

Sam was determined to have a pleasant evening, although he did wonder why Fred invited such a volatile crowd; because they were all invited, without his and Bailey's knowledge, Sam felt wary of each relative, Fred included.

It was as if Fred's handwritten invitation to Bailey had really been a lure into a situation that reeked of danger. Like a panther in the dark, Sam sensed the disturbing undercurrents swirling around him, during what should have been a casual beginning to a long overdue vacation with his wife.

So far, the start of their lovers' holiday had been anything but casual. He had not expected their first night in San Francisco to be riddled with the petty rivalries of Bailey's kin. He was thankful they had planned a full two weeks together. From the hints of trouble brewing within the lovely walls of the Painted Lady, they would need the extra time together in order to fully unwind. He was looking forward to it.

Anticipating two weeks alone with his wife kept Sam in a good mood. He had left New Hope determined to redefine the romance in his stalled marriage, and he vowed to himself that he would rekindle those dying flames, even if it meant leaving the Painted Lady after dinner this night.

As usual, Bailey's thoughts ran along the same

lines as her husband's. She had left home in search of adventure, and now she had it. For whatever reason, Fred had set into play a puzzling experience, a dinner on the verge of becoming a hazardous incident in all their lives, an event comprising cutting words, stingy attitudes, and combined speculation about the reason they were having dinner together at all. If there was any true love in the room, it was the love shared between her and Sam. It was an unsettling thought.

"I doubt we'll struggle for something to say during dinner," Bailey said under her breath to Sam.

In tune with Bailey's most private moods, Sam was immediately aware of her shift in demeanor, that subtle switch from alarm to excitement. He grinned. One thing he loved about his wife was her ability to tackle a problem with relish.

He might not have always been happy in his marriage, but he had never been bored. Bailey always found a way to keep their love new, and this getaway vacation was his way of saying thank you to the woman he loved more than he loved himself.

"Oh, it ought to be interesting, all right," Sam said. "Dexter is trying to beat Sybil to the bourbon bottle."

Fred ushered them all into the dining room. His attitude bordered on a child's delight the night before Christmas. "My cook kept things simple tonight."

"You've got the best cook on Dark Hill," Tyra said. "I don't know what we're having for dinner, but my mouth is already watering."

Fred gave her shoulder a little squeeze. "Second best cook."

Tyra smiled. "That's right, Bailey's here." She

turned to her cousin. "Will you be making anything special for us this weekend?"

Bailey blinked twice. "This weekend?"

Tyra lowered her eyes, but her tone was edged in malice. "Oh, didn't Uncle Fred tell you? I'm spending a long weekend here. I told him I needed to relax, and he told me to come on down. I came on down."

Bailey was finally put out with Fred, but since it was his house, she was determined to be polite. There was no reason she and Sam had to stay longer than a night. The object of their visit was to spend time with her uncle. After dinner, that goal would be accomplished, and they could mosey on down the California coastline, their souls and minds intent one upon the other.

"About dinner?" Tyra said.

"I suppose I could make a meal," Bailey said, "but I hadn't planned on cooking." She turned to Fred. "I hope you don't have something like this planned for the whole weekend. Sam and I would like to take you out for dinner before we leave."

Fred nodded, then motioned for her to take a seat at the table. On a side buffet, there were silver-covered warming dishes of food. "After tonight, we can play it by ear. Both my cook and my secretary have the weekend off, so I'm roughing it so to speak."

Phoebe, a petite woman with latte-colored skin and auburn hair, spoke to the room at large. "We should all be so lucky." Her sarcasm rang loud and clear.

"Having a full-time cook and secretary are my version of retirement," Fred said.

Sam eyed Bailey's uncle with wary speculation. The word *retirement* made him wonder if Fred had assembled the family together to make an announcement about his business. Knowing how poorly the family got along, Sam figured Fred probably had to resort to subterfuge just to get everyone together at one time, under one roof.

Since Bailey lived the farthest, it was possible that her uncle had sent her the special handwritten invitation to make sure she understood his request was more than a casual one. "Are you still going to your office every day?" Sam asked.

"Yep," Fred said. "I'm not into gardening or bridge or anything else. I like to work and so that's what I do."

Sybil said, low and throaty, "You like counting all that lovely money."

"Doesn't hurt," Fred said, his manner surprisingly cheerful in the tension-filled dining room. He rubbed his hands together. "Let's eat, everybody."

Within minutes, everyone had plates filled with stuffed veal breast and brown gravy, spinach with mushrooms, baked tomatoes, and cloverleaf dinner rolls. For dessert, there was a three-layer white cake, smothered in coconut, topped with mandarin oranges.

Everyone sat down. Bailey found it strange that no dates or spouses were present at the dinner table. Of all the cousins, she was the only one married.

Bailey felt fortunate to have Sam beside her. He was tough enough to protect her if necessary, smart enough to use his height and strength with care. Sam was not a man given to harsh words or behavior in his business or personal relationships, for which she was thankful. As always, his strength reinforced her own.

Quiet, supportive, he was everything she needed in a room filled with people who should have at least been friends; instead, they were barely polite, and Bailey wondered why, especially when they were all adults. It was true they had not been raised together as children, but they had been around one another enough to develop a rapport with one another; only, they never had, not really.

Perhaps that was why Bailey felt so rattled; while conversation flowed all around her, she had the weird feeling something bad was about to happen. She hoped she was wrong, but based on the animosity being displayed at the dinner table, little would surprise her this night.

Sybil was the first to enjoy the cake. Her attitude was highly sensual. Her lashes matched the smooth darkness of her thin, manicured brows. She had the athletic build common to the Durham women, including Bailey.

There was nothing too thin on Sybil. She was stacked and proud, and she wore her sexuality like a transparent glove. No longer aimed at Sam, Sybil's come-hither attitude was definitely overkill. She focused her attention on Grant.

"I heard through the grapevine you're going to lease one of Uncle Fred's buildings to warehouse some of your business inventory," she said. "Is that true?"

Grant, a hazelnut-colored man of medium height and build, took his time answering Sybil's question. "It's true."

"That's perfect," Tyra said.

Grant ignored Tyra, but continued to stare at Sybil. "How did you know about the lease of the building, Sybil? I know Fred didn't tell you."

Sybil flicked a casual look in Grant's direction. "Like I said, I heard it through the grapevine."

Fred interrupted. "Don't worry, Sybil, the building is a mess. Grant's doing me a favor by fixing it up."

"A favor?" Sybil's voice ended on a high note. She was far from pleased about this conversation. She had asked Fred for a loan to catch up her bills, and he had refused. Now, he was letting Grant lease a building for next to nothing.

"Yep," Fred said, as if oblivious to Sybil's consternation. "Grant's making renovations in lieu of rent."

Dexter, similar to Grant in color and build, spoke in a voice so deep it rumbled around the room. "How long will this . . . arrangement last?" He was almost pouting when he said it. Fred had not leased him the same building when he wanted to open a disco with friends; Dexter had in mind a sort of Studio 54. There were enough professional athletes and film industry entertainers around to make the idea feasible. Fred had simply laughed at the concept.

"Can't you see Uncle Fred is getting off on all this drama?" Phoebe said. "We all want something from him, something he refuses. What do you want, Bailey?"

"To enjoy my weekend, starting with this dinner."

"God, I don't know how you stand yourself," Sybil said. "Even as a kid you were too damned good to be true."

Sam was ready to quit the room. He rose from his seat, preparing to retire for the evening. He did not have to say a word, his expression said it all: He had reached his limit with the Durhams, Fred included.

The way Sam saw it, Bailey's relatives were spoiled, self-centered, and ungrateful. He felt as if he were in a very bad television sitcom, where everybody made rude remarks about everybody else. He did not understand why Fred allowed it, but the Painted Lady was not Sam's house. As long as Bailey could hang, so would he, but spending the night in a hotel was very appealing at the moment.

Fred read the Walkers' near-departure perfectly. He sought to stall them. "The fog is dense tonight, which means driving visibility will be poor. Anyone who wishes to stay over until morning is welcome."

Dressed in a red dress and gold hoop earrings dangling almost to her shoulders, Tyra pondered the invitation with a deliberateness that belied her flip attitude. Either she was truly afraid to drive home in heavy fog or she had nothing better to do than stir the pot at Fred's dining room table. She opted to stir the pot. "I'll stay."

"Splendid," Fred said.

"So will I," Dexter said.

"Not me," Phoebe said. "If it's time to go, it's time to go. Besides, I didn't bring a change of clothes, and I hate going home in the morning in the same outfit I left in. That is definitely uncool."

Sybil's laugh was genuine. The bourbon in her glass spilled on the white linen tablecloth, its stain as dark as the dismay on Bailey's face. "Since when have you ever cared about the neighbors?"

"My preference isn't for the neighbors' good opinion about me, it's for my good opinion about myself," Phoebe said.

Bailey rolled her eyes. "You guys are nuts."

Fred chortled in tremendous delight, as if the cattiness going on around him was the best entertainment he had had in a very long time. "Now, now, everyone, let's not get out of hand."

In the dining room, the serving table was nearly empty of food. Dexter walked over to the table, helped himself to the last of the dessert. "Fred is right. What must Sam and Bailey think of us all? We're acting like children, rotten ones at that. And you, Uncle Fred, are having way too much fun. Why did you gather us all together anyway? You know we don't get along worth beans. What gives? Is it your will?"

Disgusted, Bailey gasped. "Dexter!"

Back in his seat, Sam was as silent as the fog rolling in over the Painted Lady—silent and just as deadly. He was not exactly brooding, but he was not inclined to camouflage his feelings with a polite face either. Dexter was right. What reason did Fred have to summon such disparate people together, even if they were blood kin, other than to discuss some critical family issue, either business or personal?

Dexter's brow shot up. "Don't sound so shocked, Bailey. You had to wonder for yourself why Fred called you up here out of the blue. You didn't know the rest of us were invited, did you?"

She stole a glance at Fred. "No, I didn't."

"It hardly matters at this point why everyone is here," Sam said. "We are."

Dexter did a Marx Brothers' wiggle with his brow. "So you can talk after all. I thought for a minute you were one of those marble statues in Fred's garden."

Sam chose not to even look at Dexter, so he missed the cold gleam in the other man's eyes. "What matters is that come morning, at least some of us will be having breakfast together, at this same table. I propose we maintain a truce between now and noon tomorrow. By then, the fog should be lifted, and even if it hasn't cleared completely, the sun will be out, and driving will go much better than it will tonight."

Bailey placed a hand on her husband's forearm. "Sam's right. Since dinner is pretty much over, I suggest the rest of you figure out where you'll sleep tonight. Sam and I have the blue room upstairs."

"Who died and left you in charge?" Phoebe asked. "Uncle Fred should be the one to call off dinner and order us to bed like the spoiled children we're behaving like tonight."

Fred opened his palms in a show of goodwill. "I have no hostess tonight, so Bailey stepping into that role doesn't bother me."

"Little Miss Homemaker," Dexter said. "Of course you don't mind."

Sam pushed his chair away from the table, then extended his hand to his wife. She joined him and bid her cousins and uncle good night.

A muscle jerked in the broad column of Sam's throat. He spoke to Bailey on their way up the old spiral staircase, its polished wood feeling cool and slick beneath his fingers, as cool and slick as Fred Durham's methods for bringing his clan together. Sam's voice was gruff. "Bailey, we can spend the night in a hotel, fog or no fog."

"I know, but Dexter's right. Fred is up to something. There's no way he should have enjoyed the fireworks going on tonight, but he did. His eyes were dancing, and he barely touched his food."

"I noticed he didn't answer Dexter's question about his will," Sam said.

"Oh, yeah," Bailey said. Her frown was deep,

her eyes perplexed. "I forgot about that. You think his omission is important?"

Sam drew a heavy breath, then released it slowly. "I do."

"Why?"

"Your invitation. The fact we didn't know the others were coming, even though they knew you were coming."

Bailey had a sudden urge to run, but she squelched the desire. This was her uncle's home, and she had always been welcome here. She just wished she could shake the feeling of dread.

She said, "Funny how the Painted Lady feels a bit creepy now that it's dark and I know the fog has pretty much made visibility zero outside. I'd forgotten how incredibly thick the fog can be this close to the bay. I bet flights are shut down at the airport as well. We're safer here than on the road looking for a hotel anyway, but tomorrow is a different story, tomorrow, we can move on."

"I agree," Sam said. "If we wake up to the same mess we had to deal with tonight, we're leaving. I don't want any more drama until I get back to the office and hear about whatever went wrong while I was gone."

Bailey beamed at him. "I can't believe you left your pager and cell phone at home. Thank you."

"I promised you two full weeks of my time, and I intend to give it to you, Bailey. You've got your cell phone, so if my parents or the girls need us, they can reach us. I'm not worried about anyone else."

"Me neither."

"Good," Sam said, his tone distracted. For a woman he had been intimate with on every level, Bailey still had the power to plunge his senses into romantic chaos, and for this, he was thankful. He considered himself a lucky man. Breathing deeply, Sam savored her perfume, the scent of her hair, her breath, her skin.

What had happened in the dining room less than an hour before felt like old news. Inside the bedroom they would share together, at least for one night, his thoughts and feelings rested solely on her. Despite the drama going on beyond their bedroom doors, Sam was glad they had left New Hope and their normal routine, at least for a little while.

In turn, the lusty gleam in Bailey's eyes was hardly masked by the downward sweep of her dusky lashes. She knew her husband wanted her, knew that deep down, there were disturbing waters of unrest teeming below the surface of his desire.

He may have temporarily dismissed the madness of the dining room, but he had not forgotten. When their romantic interlude reached its zenith for the evening, when their bodies were slick with sweat, their flesh sated with passion, his mind would return to the sinister feeling the Painted Lady had taken on once the fog had rolled in after their arrival that afternoon, the fog's density binding Fred Durham's guests by an uneasy truce that would extend from now until breakfast the next day.

As she eased into the warmth of Sam's embrace, into the healing rituals of their unique brand of lovers' play, Bailey was almost able to force away the chill roving down her spine, almost.

THREE

Morning arrived, still heavy with fog. Bailey stood at the guest bedroom window, which overlooked the side yard, a narrow affair bordered in orange Tropicana roses. Normally Bailey would be able to smell the roses from the open window if it were not for the fog. It was as if the fog cloaked sight as well as scent.

As high on Dark Hill as the Painted Lady sat, the view would normally appear limitless, but today, Bailey could scarcely see the paint on the windowsill. She hoped the fog would dissipate soon, so that she and Sam could continue their journey; during the night, they had decided that a hotel was preferable to spending another night with her uncle in the Painted Lady.

Had it not been for the warring relatives, Bailey would have enjoyed the dense fog. It cooled the air and softened the leaves of the trees and shrubs in her yard at home by adding moisture and dampening the soil; it had worked that same kind of magic on the evergreen shrubs in her uncle's formal gardens.

Thinking of home made Bailey feel a bit melan-

SACRED LOVE   47

choly, a little homesick, and she still had two weeks
of vacation to go. If she went home now, the girls
would be as disappointed as Sam, who moved
about the bedroom, its space lightly scattered with
their discarded clothing from the night before.

"It's crazy the way it can be sunny one day, cold
and wet the next," he said. "The temperature outside must be in the midsixties, if that."

Bailey turned to face him. "Here we are, in California, the Sunshine State, and we're trapped inside a one-hundred-plus-year-old Victorian house,
draped in fog, on a hillside that, for the moment
at least, is hidden away from the rest of the world.
Crazy."

Sam eased his arms around Bailey, his chest to
her back. Together, they studied the fog, their
manner as subdued and affected as if it rained and
the roads leading toward and away from the
Painted Lady were flooded, making it difficult, if
not impossible to leave. "I suppose big scary
houses aren't limited to the East Coast or the
southern states," Sam said, "but I hear you.
There's something unsettling about it not being
safe to leave home."

Bailey turned in his arms, her face lifted to his.
"Speaking of home, are you sorry you came?"

"No."

Oh, how she loved him. Never had Sam been
more comforting to Bailey than he was right now.
His eyes, dark and fine, showed a sensitivity to her
moods and thoughts. If nothing else, this trip had
reopened her eyes to the basic goodness that lived
in Sam.

After the birth of their daughters, Sam's love
had matured along with his sense of accountability.
Because of his increased sense of duty, he had in-

sisted Bailey stay home to raise their daughters, even though it had been difficult financially, especially when the girls were small, but in the long run, they both were thankful they had chosen solidarity over the security of dual incomes. As parents, it had been a tough, but rewarding struggle.

Even now, the money Bailey earned from catering went into savings and retirement funds. Once the girls were grown and living in homes of their own, she and Sam planned to travel together, their reward for sticking by each other through the lean years and the fat ones. This trip to San Francisco, rocky as it began, was a promise for them both of the good things in their relationship that were yet to come.

Bailey cupped her husband's face, its image one of pride and strength, then pulled him toward her and kissed him. He tightened his embrace, as together, they prepared to face the rest of the Durham family: It was time for breakfast.

On the way to the stairs, Bailey said, "I almost forgot. Last night, Uncle Fred said he wanted to walk down with us to breakfast. I just need to knock on his door."

She knocked three times. "Uncle Fred?" There was no answer.

Sam frowned. "Looks like he's down already."

"No. He said specifically that he wanted us to go down at the same time. He has to be in there."

"He's probably asleep, Bailey."

"He gets up at five every day. He says it's his best time to think and look over business papers. It's eight now."

This time, Sam knocked on Fred's door, but it was Bailey who turned the doorknob, made of burgundy hued cloisonné. She wondered idly how much such a thing would cost in an antique store. So many of the details in Fred's home were understated in their simplicity, like the doorknob, yet remarkable in detail and design. She wished she and Sam were staying after breakfast so that she could explore the Painted Lady and ask her uncle questions about the items that interested her.

"Bailey," Sam said, "don't open that door."

"Maybe he's sick."

"Bailey?" Sam's tone held a warning note.

"You can turn your back if you want."

"Give me a break."

She laughed softly. She pushed open the door, a heavy structure made of rosewood, imported from the Far East when John Durham built the Painted Lady.

The bed was made. Seeing this, Sam said, "I told you, busybody. He's downstairs or maybe he's in his study."

Bailey walked farther into the room. "Uncle Fred?"

Sam was just about to grab her by the arm to pull her back when he noticed Fred's clothing and shoes, as if they were set out fresh that very morning, over the back of a dark leather chair. It was unusual, but Sam felt his skin prickle with misgiving. Bailey's gasp at the bathroom door did not surprise him.

"Sam! He's . . . dead."

His heart heavy, Sam joined Bailey at the open door of the huge bathroom. It was true. Fred Durham lay in a tub of bathwater, probably dead by electrocution. In his lap was a handheld blowdryer.

In shock, Bailey lost the ability to move or breathe. She was rooted to the rug on the bathroom floor, her eyes wide and her mouth hanging open.

Sam took charge of his wife and of the moment. There was nothing anyone could do for Fred now. "Let's alert the others and then call the police."

As Bailey leaned on him, Sam led her away from the bathroom, out the bedroom door, and down the stairs to the first floor. Through the windows of the Painted Lady, the fog was thick as ever, its presence ominous.

FOUR

Detective Hark Bittersweet was tall, dark, and deadly serious. He worked hard, rarely played, and seldom trusted anybody, regardless of first impressions. His first impression of Sam and Bailey Walker was good.

His impression was good because the husband supported his wife by standing close without touching, his manner protective without being overbearing. In the detective's mind, their behavior was that of a couple secure in their relationship, neither of them particularly needy, neither overly frightened because one was there to comfort the other.

The couple's closeness stood out in the parlor, a roomful of nervous, distraught, yet greedy relatives, a greed that was evident in the hawkish looks presented to the detective; no one wanted to be considered a suspect of any wrongdoing prior to Fred's accident, and yet no one was anxious to leave the premises. The detective trusted no one.

Like Hark, Sam trusted no one at the Victorian mansion on Dark Hill either. His position, as bodyguard to his wife, was as evident as the dead body in the bathtub.

The detective shifted his gaze from Sam to

Bailey. His eyes missed nothing. Bailey did not fidget, nor did she offer comfort to any of her cousins. It was as if she had antennae going in all directions: to Phoebe, who stared out a window, her expression unreadable; to Dexter, who paced the room endlessly, his feet silent against the ornate, imported carpets; to Tyra, who sat in a Queen Anne chair, her arms and legs crossed, the skin beneath her left eye twitching uncontrollably; to Grant, who never once left the bourbon bottle, his expression one of an angry man; and to Sybil, who inspected each of her fingernails as if she had never seen them before.

Perhaps, the detective reasoned, they were all a little bit angry at the suddenness of Fred's death, at the many questions presented by the way he died. Fred Durham was old, had lived a long and productive life, so on one hand the suspects were accepting, and on the other hand, the family very obviously had the blues. The man, after all, had been their uncle.

The man had also been incredibly rich; the chandelier in the foyer was real crystal as were many of the knobs on the doors. There was authentic Italian marble on the floors. Deep red velvet covered the windows from ceiling to floor. Fred's furnishings cost a fine and pretty penny.

Hark Bittersweet knew all about interior design for celebrity homes; his ex-wife, Stella, had been a designer. She left him to make her own way and fortune in the City of Angels: Los Angeles, California.

Stella had used him to get her education. She used her education to network. She networked to gain prestigious clients. She worked with newly rich gangster rappers and rising movie stars and film directors.

Hark believed Stella ruined him in a lot of ways, most of them mental, so that when he looked at the tears in Bailey's eyes, the detective was skeptical. Her tears could have been as genuine as the crystal in the chandelier or fake as the faux diamonds around Sybil's neck. Time would tell.

Meanwhile, Bailey was the detective's prime suspect, her husband was not. The detective figured that a man as big and powerful as Sam had no need to fry an old man in the bathtub. A lady might do that though, the detective reasoned.

Bailey was small, Fred a big man, despite his advanced age. The tub was perfect for murder because her presence in the bathroom would not have been expected. She was also first on the spot, which made it easy to explain her fingerprints at the crime scene.

Phoebe unwrapped a thin Mexican cigar, cut the tip off, sniffed the cigar, carefully lit it, and savored every particle of smoke on her tongue before she exhaled. She had been smoking cigars since she was twelve. "I can't believe the old bastard is dead."

Bailey could not believe Phoebe was so callous. "Be careful what you say and how you say it."

Phoebe blew smoke in Bailey's direction. "Why? Because Hark's here?"

"No, you idiot," Bailey said, "it's because I'm here. If nothing else, I cared more about Uncle Fred than I did his money. You can't say the same, and we both know it."

Phoebe leaned forward, legs open, elbows on her knees, eyes sharp. "Haven't seen you in years, Bailey. How do I know you and Sammy aren't having money troubles? How do I know you didn't come all the way to Frisco to squeeze cold cash from Uncle Fred's private stash?"

Bailey had the look of a woman who wanted to break someone in half. "He sent me an invitation."

Phoebe's breath was caught between a cough and a harsh snort of laughter. "Uncle Fred didn't do anything from the kindness of his heart. He either did something he needed to confess or he was about to do something he needed to confess. He didn't make millions being stupid. What did he want from you, Bailey?"

"Nothing."

"You never were a good liar, cuz. I saw you cut a quick look at Sammy."

"Sam," Bailey said. "My husband's name is Sam."

Phoebe laughed, the sound raspy from Mexican smoke. "I know what his name is." She turned to Sam. "So. Mr. Ex-ec-u-tive. What's your take on all this drama?"

"My take is that you are the most disrespectful person I've ever met."

"Ever?"

Sam stared her down.

Dexter clapped his hands. "Bravo, Sam. It's not often Phoebe gets smacked to the curb where she belongs."

Sam's top lip curled in disgust. "You people are nuts."

Dexter grunted in agreement. "We people are Bailey's people. I'm almost sorry to say, well, actually, I'm shocked to say that for once, I agree with Phoebe. Fred wasn't a casual person. He didn't just extend an invitation to you and Bailey for nothing. He wanted something. The question is what?"

Sam eyeballed the silent homicide detective, a man who took no notes, who did not confer with his crime scene technicians, who behaved like the rest of Bailey's relatives: hawkish and hard-edged. "Maybe he wanted to be with a member of the family who gave him respect."

Dexter studied the clear nail polish on his left hand. "Respect is earned. The fact that Fred has very little respect from his family says a lot about Fred the man."

"Respect is given to trustworthy people," Sam said. "If you behaved this way around Fred, I don't blame him for being 'casual' as you put it, with you all. The man was your relative. He invited you into his home, and whether you like it or not, my wife and I were made to feel welcome about coming here. I advise you people to watch what you say to us and what you say about Fred. We cared about him."

Dexter raised a brow. "Aren't you the iron type. I bet you wave a big stick at work, too. But I'll tell you something, Sam, I don't care what you want. I don't care how you feel. There's a lot of money at stake now that Fred's gone. Hark is here to see our individual reactions. If I behaved any differently than I am right now, he'd be suspicious. Right, Hark?"

The detective was slow to respond. He visually inventoried each person in the room before opening his mouth to speak. "I agree with the Walkers. Regardless of how you felt personally about Fred, respect is warranted and deserved."

Bailey put a hand on Sam's arm. "Let's go home."

Hark interrupted. "Sorry, Mrs. Walker. I'll need you to stick around for questioning."

"You can't mean for me to stay in this house," Bailey said.

"I do."

"Why?"

Dexter flashed perfect white teeth. "He thinks you did it."

Hark explained. "The death is suspicious. Because the victim was wealthy and of sound mind I want to rule out any possibility of foul play."

Bailey looked as if she wanted to strike the detective. "You can't be serious? I received an invitation."

"You received an opportunity."

"To kill an eighty-seven-year-old man? Give me a break!"

Distaste for the detective was stamped all over Sam's face. A quick glance through the parlor window indicated the fog had only thickened. They were safer in the Painted Lady than on the narrow, winding streets of Dark Hill. "We'll stay the weekend. We're in one of the guest bedrooms. If you want us to stay longer, you'll have to charge Bailey with some crime. Obviously, you think she stands to inherit his money."

"That's ridiculous," Bailey said.

Hark was shaking his head before she finished talking. "Actually, it isn't. You can see from Phoebe and Dexter's behavior that there were problems between them. Fred might have selected a surviving relative that he felt the most kinship with and offered that person his entire estate."

"This is absurd," Bailey said.

"I hope so," Hark said.

Bailey stalked to the guest bedroom she shared

with Sam. "I'm ashamed to admit I'm related to those people. Next they'll be saying the butler did it!"

Sam pulled her into his arms, his chin resting against her forehead. He used his hands to caress her back. "I find it interesting that nobody is taking Fred's death at face value. Just because he was rich doesn't mean someone in the family killed him for his money. He's a huge philanthropist, very giving. He was also old and maybe lonely. Maybe he had an accident. Maybe he committed suicide. I don't know what to think."

"Just hold me, Sam."

Almost absentmindedly, Sam squeezed his wife tighter, his thoughts focused on solving Fred's mysterious death. "We both know you're innocent of anything wrong, but as Hark pointed out, money provides motive, the invitation provides opportunity, the electrocution the method of death, and like he also said, Fred's death was easy to carry off by someone he trusted."

Bailey pushed back in order to gaze into her husband's face. "He wouldn't trust me in the bathroom with him. The man was buck naked, Sam. He didn't have enough hair on his head to warrant a blow-dryer. What was an eighty-seven-year-old man doing with a blow-dryer in the bathtub?"

"That's probably why Detective Bittersweet is suspicious of foul play."

"Can't say I blame him, but Phoebe and Dexter were the ones showing out the most."

"Phoebe and Dexter live in San Francisco. They could have killed Fred anytime."

"I can't think about this, Sam."

"You have to think about it, Bailey."

"It's a nightmare."

"Someone in your family might be guilty of murder. Phoebe and Dexter are such obvious suspects that Hark is giving them only a cursory inspection."

Bailey rubbed her arms, even though they were not cold. "He doesn't strike me as a man who ignores any kind of detail. I don't think he discounts Phoebe and Dexter because he's accustomed to their animosity. I think he's trying to get a handle on us. Aside from Fred's accident, we're the part of the picture that doesn't fit. I can't blame the detective for being cautious. I just wish he'd spend the time he's spending on us, looking somewhere else."

Sam's voice was troubled. "I think it's strange that in a city this big, a homicide detective is on close terms with the Durham family. Don't you?"

"Not really," Bailey said. "The Bittersweets live on Dark Hill. Rumor has it that the only time Fred came close to marrying, it was to a Bittersweet. Hark is probably here out of a sense of loyalty."

"Fred never mentioned them, and we talked a lot whenever we were together."

Bailey shrugged. "We didn't talk about our friends either on the few occasions we saw Fred. I don't think it's unusual."

"Do you think Fred's death was accidental?"

"Of course I do."

Sam shook his head. "The blow-dryer doesn't fit."

"I agree about the blow-dryer," Bailey said, "but who knows what he was doing?"

"Most children know not to use appliances in the tub or shower. A grown man would definitely know this. Fred was practically bald. All he had to do was dry his head with a towel."

Bailey spoke slowly, as if what she was thinking was too horrendous to speak out loud. "Okay, supposing his death wasn't accidental. You can't possibly think it was suicide."

"No," Sam said. "Fred was too proud and well grounded for that."

"Okay, then you think he was . . . murdered?"

Sam was grim. "If you rule out accident and suicide then, yes."

"That's crazy."

"I don't think so, Bailey. Not after Dexter and Phoebe's attitude this afternoon. They were outrageous. I was disgusted with them both."

"So was I, but that doesn't mean they killed my uncle."

"Your uncle was rich."

Bailey threw her hands in the air. "He's always been rich."

Sam's tone was grave. "He hasn't always been old. What if Fred called you here to make an announcement about his will?"

"I'd be surprised."

"Okay, but do you think it's possible?"

"Of course I do, Sam. Anything's possible."

"Yeah, but you're also the last surviving Durham. Your sister was adopted as a baby. The Painted Lady has always belonged to a blooded Durham."

Bailey frowned. "Dexter and Phoebe are as entitled to this property as I am."

"Yes and no," Sam said. "They're relatives, yes, but by marriage to a Durham. You're a direct descendent of John Durham, the first family millionaire. If your dad was alive, this property probably would have been left to him. You have no brothers, and so, logically, the house would go to you. We both know that Fred was very into family lineage. In fact, for him, family lineage was an obsession. It's from him that I heard the term 'blooded Durham.' "

"It could work out that way, but Uncle Fred was a big philanthropist. He could easily have left his fortune to charity. The Painted Lady is only one aspect of his wealth. The carriage business was the backbone. He was also successful in stocks."

Sam prowled the bedroom. "I'm just looking for a way to make sense out of what's happened. It can't be an accident that you were invited to visit. It can't be an accident the blow-dryer was in the bathtub with Fred. Of all the people who could be here investigating Fred's death, the one person controlling the investigation is somehow connected to the Durham family. I'd say that's a conflict of interest."

"I would too," Bailey said, "but maybe it's a good thing. Hark Bittersweet is every bit as suspicious of Fred's death as we are."

"But he wasn't quizzing Dexter and Phoebe. I'm worried he won't look any farther than you for a suspect."

"You keep alluding to murder."

"It fits, Bailey. Think about it. Based on my personality, if I were found dead in the bathtub from electrocution with a blow-dryer, wouldn't you think I was murdered?"

"Only because nothing else would fit, not even an accident."

"We have to think objectively here, Bailey. It's hardest for you because Fred was your uncle, but my thinking isn't clouded by the same emotions you're feeling. I cared about Fred, but I'm not emotionally connected to him the way you are. Besides, the way it stands now, I'm the only person in your corner."

"You don't know that."

Sam pushed his point home. "Detective Bittersweet doesn't want you to leave just yet. I see that as pretty specific and pretty disturbing. I won't allow you to be railroaded. We'll stay until funeral arrangements are made, but that's it."

"Well, I suppose it's a good thing we already planned an extended vacation. The girls will be all right where they are, and of course we have to tell them what happened but we might as well stay a few days until this mess is all cleared up."

Sam lay on his back on the bed, then pulled Bailey on top of him. "Come here, sweetheart. You're rambling."

Bailey raised up on her elbows so she could look at him. "I'm scared, Sam. All your suspicions are so on target. I feel selfish for thinking about how Uncle Fred's death will affect my future."

"Fred is beyond our help."

"Not if he was murdered. If so, it's our responsibility to figure out who did it."

Sam flipped Bailey onto her back; then it was his turn to raise up on his elbows while they talked. "That's Detective Bittersweet's job. I'm going to make sure he does it."

"Let's find out why Dexter and Phoebe are really here," Bailey said. "Maybe if we know that, we'll have some clue about Uncle Fred's state of mind before he died."

"Good idea."

"But you want to know something, Sam? Something weird?"

"What?"

"After I accepted his invitation, Uncle Fred said

I was worth more than a million before we hung up. What if he knew he was going to die?"

"It's a very real possibility," Sam said. "Fred could have been terminally ill. Cancer wouldn't be out of the norm for his age group. Neither would some other type of system failure in his body."

"He said he was old. He didn't say he was sick. The strange thing is that he didn't look or sound as if something was wrong."

Sam eased off Bailey so that they lay side by side in each other's arms. "The autopsy done on him will determine the actual facts concerning his physical health."

"I hope it'll also provide a clue about why he was using a blow-dryer before he could even get out of the bathtub. Matter of fact, I'd like to know why he had a blow-dryer at all. Like you pointed out, Fred was mostly bald."

"Don't worry, baby," Sam said. "We'll get all the answers we need. Every last one."

"I hope you're right. If Detective Bittersweet really does decide I'm guilty of murder, I don't know what I'll do."

The look on Sam's face was nothing nice. "You'll fight."

FIVE

Hark Bittersweet was in his late forties and had been on the San Francisco police force long enough to retire. In seven days he planned to do exactly that, early enough to enjoy his good health and the money he had saved to travel around the world.

He wanted to see it all, the deserts of Africa, the mountains of India, the Australian outback, the cathedrals of Spain, the South Pacific, the rivers of Brazil, and then take a break in the United States to tour the icebergs of Alaska.

In his travels, he planned to work just enough to earn his keep. For him, there would be no more strict schedules or routine paperwork, which had been his lot during his twenty years spent as an officer of the law. Hark's entire life had been structured for success and material gain. After his first and only marriage to a greedy, grasping, materialistic woman, he wanted the simple life.

For Hark, the simple life meant having just enough clothes and personal items to fit inside a small suitcase or perhaps a large backpack, the type worn by the most serious outdoorsmen, like hikers and mountain climbers.

He wanted to wake up in the morning and really

see it, the sun slowly rising, the gradual warming of the air as dawn eased into early morning. He wanted to . . . solve the mysterious death of Fred Durham—in seven days.

He felt he was qualified to deal with the Durham relatives, his experience with greedy, grasping, manipulative people fine-tuned by the years spent with his ex-wife. Where his other colleagues might have been swayed by the wealth and prestige of the Durham name, thus turning a tolerant eye toward their eccentricities, Hark knew that he would not. He felt that he alone was the best man for the job at hand.

Besides his personal qualifications for the job, the detective wanted no unsolved cases on his conscience when he retired. That Fred Durham was a Bittersweet family friend was significant to him; perhaps he might have accepted that every case would not be solved before he retired, but he could not do that, not when the Bittersweet integrity was at stake.

The Bittersweets admired honor and discipline, the driving reason behind three generations of Bittersweets who studied and practiced law enforcement. The detective felt compelled to figure out what happened to Fred.

He felt little need to delve beyond the immediate Durham household to find Fred's killer; at no time had Hark considered his friend's death a suicide. In addition to the relatives assembled in the Painted Lady at the time of Fred's death, there were two other suspects: Fred's secretary and his cook.

Fred hired a gardening service, not a full-time groundskeeper, and there was no butler. When someone knocked on Fred's door, he answered it himself when his secretary was away for the day. On the night of Fred's death, the cook was off duty and the secretary had gone home.

It was Bailey who captured his interest. She did not fit with the rest of the Durham clan, at least not in an obvious way. She was not particularly rude, she did not appear to need anything, and yet there she was being feisty with Phoebe and Dexter less than an hour after Fred's body had been found; she had appeared shocked by the death, but not devastated.

Thinking hard on the subject, the detective realized that Bailey had almost a clinical approach to the entire unfortunate incident. It was her detachment the detective found intriguing. Why was it that Hark had never met Bailey or her husband, Sam, until now?

It was ironic that the first time they should meet, it was under death-related circumstances, and yet Bailey had the most composure of all the relatives, including her husband, who looked ready to fight anyone who stepped within a foot of his wife's face without his permission.

The detective made a mental note to ask Bailey for the original invitation. Why was it that only she claimed to have received a written missive when the other relatives claimed a phone call? That alone made her stand out.

It was possible that she wanted the police to think she had truly legitimate business at the Painted Lady, and if that was the case, she most definitely had something to hide, but what? The most common denominator between the relatives, aside from being rude, was their open bid for money.

Hark recognized that the only way he was going

to get fast results was if he had a clear objective and a solid method of achieving that goal. What did he want? An open-and-shut case. What stood in the way? The facts.

It was up to Hark to sift through his impressions, to reconstruct a chronology of events before and after Fred Durham's death, and to ascertain whether or not Fred's death was truly accidental.

Accidents happened. Accidents ranked number four in the top five leading causes of death in every age group in the United States. In the detective's experience, accidental deaths, both sudden and unexpected, drew intense and immediate emotional responses from family members, but not so in the case of Fred Durham. In this instance, accidental death served as a spotlight on a highly dysfunctional family.

Hark had much to do in a very short time if he planned to retire without an unsolved case as his last investigation. It was normal in a city the size of San Francisco to have open homicide investigations, but pride would not let him end his professional career on a sour note.

After all, the Bittersweets and the Durhams were two of the oldest families on Dark Hill, and in an odd twist of fate, Hark had been appointed the principal investigator on the case. He felt honor bound, morally and professionally, to tackle the case of Fred's death with every skill and resource he had at his disposal. It was his job to determine the truth.

Accident, suicide, or murder, what had happened to Fred? Electrocution was an explainable accident, an unusual homicide, and a difficult murder to prove. Hark had checked the blow-dryer at the death scene; it was a standard 110-volt.

Electric shock would change the normal electrical pattern of Fred's heart: His being surprised in the nude would make his heart quiver but not stop it from pumping blood. Without quick restoration of circulation by CPR or by defibrillator, the heart would go into cardiac arrest and death would be imminent. This had probably happened to Fred.

Anyone could have thrown the blow-dryer into his bathtub. If the victim had been unsuspecting, perhaps shocked and briefly incapacitated, murder could have been done easily and cleanly.

The blow-dryer would generate a deadly cardiac arrhythmia without a serious outward sign of injury. There would have been no burning, no internal or external tissue damage, no visible disfigurement, no blood, no mess to physically touch by the killer.

Anyone could have done it: the secretary, the cook, the relatives, anyone, including the victim himself.

SIX

It was Saturday morning, the fog and Fred's guests were still present at the Painted Lady. Because the environment was hostile, Sam stuck close to Bailey's side, and for this, she was thankful. The last thing she wanted to be was alone.

She accepted his presence as she would a guardian angel, someone always close, always on guard, never failing in his duty. Secure in her safety, Bailey paced through the mansion, visiting each room that was open to her as she carefully got the layout of the house together in her mind.

While she paced, Sam remained silent, his manner slightly ominous because he said nothing; his brow, normally smooth, was wrinkled in concentration. He believed that the safest plan of action was to take his wife away from the drama, let the police handle the investigation of Fred's death, but this, he could not do. He was leery of the officer in charge of investigating Fred's case.

Sam had hoped he and Bailey would never be involved in a death situation again, but here they were, in an old house, on a fog-enshrouded hill, in a city as known for its great history and food as it was known for its murder mysteries and other sinister secrets . . . such as what was going on within the ranks of the Durham family.

Perhaps if Sam had never been involved in a murder, he might not be so suspicious of Fred's accident, but Sam was suspicious and once that door of distrust was open in his mind, it would take solid proof of an accidental death to close it.

They entered the parlor.

The parlor was a pivotal point in the house. In the parlor, the Durham clan gathered to mingle, to argue, to keep each within the other's accusing sight. Two full living room sets dominated the living space. There was a fireplace, but candelabras, tall and ornate silver ones, served as a focal point in the lavishly decorated room.

With the clack of pointed heels against the bare spots on the hardwood floors, Tyra entered the too-quiet parlor. "What a way to start the weekend," she said.

Bailey scanned her cousin. The younger woman wore a salmon-colored tank top with a matching pair of slacks. Standing beside Bailey, who was dressed all in cream, they could have been two wealthy women on their way to browse one exclusive boutique after another in one of the upscale shops in downtown San Francisco.

"Haven't seen you since the family reunion six years ago," Bailey said. "You look the same."

"Thank you."

Sam moved easily among the tension-filled room and its brittle-nerved occupants as if he were a news reporter—confident, quiet, determined. He wore his power with the casual grace of a large cat, his manner contemplative, as if considering the best way to defend his territory, and for Sam, that territory was Bailey. He joined her, club sodas in hand, one for himself, another for her.

Bailey turned her head slightly, enough to gaze at him, briefly, her lovely brown eyes entirely unreadable to anyone other than Sam. He alone knew that anger rested beneath the surface of her watchful demeanor.

He said softly, "I love you."

She laid her hand over his forearm. She felt strange, as if Fred might appear at any moment, to explain away the confusion. Talk of a will just prior to his death hung in the household air like the smell of rotten fish. With Fred's property, investments, and other assets valued in the multimillions, those hasty words were more than rude, they were revealing. They showed a collective hunger for money, a classic motive for murder.

In order to solve the mystery, Bailey could not afford to let sentiment obstruct her clear vision. Clear vision meant focusing on the details, breaking her feelings and instincts into meaning and reason.

She first considered the issue of timing. The timing of Fred's death was too convenient: Everyone had the same alibi—one another, everyone had the same motive—greed; everyone had the same opportunity—an invitation to ride out the fog at the Painted Lady for one night.

The word *invitation* kept popping up: Bailey's printed invitation, her cousins' verbal invitations, Fred's open suggestion for everyone to share his home for one night. Had he planned to invite them to spend the night all along, or had he simply taken advantage of Mother Nature? Round and round, Bailey considered the possibilities, hoping for some clue that was so obvious, it stared her in the face.

While Bailey refuted sentiment, her eyes focusing on the melting cubes in her crystal glass, Sam went one step further by refuting the idea of coincidence. He believed nothing in life was random, and that even an "accident" had a series of events leading to its cause, then away toward its effect. Fred was the beginning, the middle, and the end of the disaster going on around them.

Sam sat with Bailey on a sofa, rage flaring hard and bright inside him. This was supposed to be a fresh start for their relationship, a turning point in their marriage. Their union had endured the weathering effects of a first and second mortgage on their home, the birth and rearing of their children, the merging of in-laws and extended families, of long absences related to work and business travel, of solving two homicides.

In Bailey, Sam had found an unflagging cheerleader. She supported his dreams, understood his vision of excellence in the workplace as well as in the New Hope, California, community in which they lived.

It was her goodness that kept him grounded as he shifted from work to home in a merry-go-round that often left him emotionally spent and sometimes disillusioned, as she was feeling right now. Sam was about to refill her glass when he heard shouts in the hallway.

Sybil was furious with Hark Bittersweet. She stomped into the parlor, poured herself a bourbon, tossed the short drink to the back of her throat, swallowed hard, wiped her hand across her bare lips, and sneered at everyone present.

"I did not kill Uncle Fred." She spoke each word precisely.

Bailey froze: At last, the unspeakable had been spoken to all. She could not find her voice, but Sam could. "Have you been accused?" He pointed his gaze at the detective, but Sam's words were only for Sybil.

"Practically."

Sybil spoke with such hatred, Sam felt Bailey stiffen beside him: Sybil's face was livid as a neon sign, her anger was so out of control. Sam thought she might snatch the velvet curtains off the windows, then rip them to shreds. She consoled herself with another drink.

For several tense moments, no one present said a word or made a move, each of them aware that Fred Durham's moment of truth was upon them: Had he been loved, reviled, or revered? Bailey suspected all three terms applied.

Whodunit?

Who pushed Fred Durham over the mental edge? Was it Tyra, lonely and desperate, perhaps in debt because she gambled too much and needed help to pay off loans?

Was it Sybil, sarcastic and rude, steady drinker and all-around gossip? Did she sound so cruel, so brutally honest because she wanted to throw the ever-watchful Detective Bittersweet off her trail?

Was it Phoebe, the ex-juvenile delinquent and irrepressible wild child? Had she finally gotten into a mess that only Fred's money could buy her out?

Was it Dexter, the perennial pretty boy, the big spender? He drove a Hummer and a classic sports car—on a young executive's salary. Was his income derived from purely legitimate means or was it supplemented by other sources, perhaps the prominent single women he dated, or even Uncle Fred?

Was it Grant, pissed off because his charismatic personality had won him the start-up money for his multiple business endeavors only to have those ventures stall and fail with no hope of repaying borrowed start-up funds? Did he push Fred over the edge to gain access to his inheritance?

Bailey sought Sam's hand. His grip was hard, calloused . . . comforting. He offered no other form of affection because none was needed. What she needed was space to think and to feel, within his circle of protection. He knew she needed time to be alone, at least mentally. Emotionally, Bailey needed to know Sam was there for her, and he was.

Despite the destructive forces pressing down on them, much like the fog pressing down on Dark Hill, Bailey never looked so beautiful . . . or so tragic. There was an oddness between them that was both surreal and fascinating to Sam.

Her brooding vulnerability drew him to her on a novel, rare level, a delicate shading of the senses based on nonverbal cues and perception rather than words. As he watched, her state of mind slipped into a distance so far away she failed to hear when he called her name.

Leaning down, Sam touched her hair with his lips, that act of grace returning her to him, refocused and alert, thrust once more into the hard, unbreakable circle of his protection. The stricken look then fled her face, and in its place was an artless love, the stuff of fables, the only love worth living and dying for: true love. Whatever silent battle Bailey had faced was over now.

Together, Sam vowed, they would forge ahead.

Together, they would fight.

Together, they would win.

SEVEN

Later that evening, Hark Bittersweet broke terrible news to the Durham relatives. They were in the parlor. "Fred was definitely murdered."

Bailey squeezed Sam's hand as she asked the detective, "How do you know?"

"There were no fingerprints on the blow-dryer."

Bailey considered the ramifications. No fingerprints suggested no one had touched the blow-dryer when obviously somebody had done that very thing. "You believe someone inside the house last night killed him?" she asked.

"Yes."

"You aren't gonna let us leave the Painted Lady, are you?"

"Not yet. There are several things to determine."

"Motive, method, and opportunity," Bailey said.

The detective raised a brow. "Yes."

Sam eyed the detective. "I think the motive was money. We all know the method and obviously the fog provided the opportunity."

Dexter spoke to no one in particular. "A real murder. Hard to believe."

The detective sighed as if he carried the weight of the world on his shoulders. "Yes."

Dexter scoffed at the detective. "You're a fountain of explanation, Hark."

The detective said nothing.

Bailey did. "There's more to figure out here than who killed Uncle Fred. With his death disclosed as a murder, it means everybody in this room is at risk."

Grant spoke for them all. "Not everybody."

The detective disagreed. "Yes, everybody."

Sam spoke up. "If money is the motive for the crime, why not kill Fred years ago? He's been rich for most of his life, and his wealth was never a secret to anybody in this room. There's been ample opportunity to do away with him. I want to know what set Fred's killer off. I also want to know to what degree the killer will be prosecuted."

"He's right," Phoebe said. "I want to know what sparked the actual murder, and I also want to know what Sam means by degree. The way I see it, dead is dead."

"I'm referring to the different classifications of murder," Sam said.

Hark provided a deeper explanation. "First-degree murder involves three key factors: planning, deliberate malice, and lack of remorse. It also applies if someone is killed while a major felony is being committed, such as burglary."

Tyra leaned forward. "Do you think somebody was trying to rob Uncle Fred?"

Hark had checked with the dead man's regular staff thoroughly. "Nothing appears to be stolen."

Sybil was intrigued. "That leaves second-degree murder then."

"Maybe," the detective said. "Second-degree murder involves malice but not premeditation. Voluntary manslaughter is when someone is killed without malice even though a killing was done on purpose."

"That makes no sense," Sybil said. She smacked her empty glass down on the nearest tabletop.

"It does actually," the detective said. "For example, if two people are fighting and one person kills the other in anger, that's voluntary manslaughter."

Dexter chose his words carefully. "So you're saying that someone could have been in the bathroom with Fred, argued with him, and chucked the blow-dryer in the tub and hoped he died?"

The detective was quick to respond. "Yes."

Bailey shook her head. "But there were no fingerprints on the murder weapon. That's premeditation."

The detective held up a hand to stop her. "That's for the courts to decide. There are other degrees of murder but none of that matters at this point in the investigation. Right now, everybody in this room is a suspect."

"Okay," Bailey said. "The crucial thing for us to do is figure out who did it."

Sam slid his arm around his wife's shoulders. "She's right. We're all suspects but we're also witnesses. By that I mean we all have seen something or heard something that might help Detective Bittersweet solve Fred's murder."

Hark eyed Sam speculatively. "I'll interview each of you until I'm satisfied with your answers to my questions."

Glass in hand, Sybil headed to the liquor bottles. "I heard nothing. Saw nothing. I was in bed."

Bailey took the bourbon bottle and glass from Sybil's hands. She returned them to the bar. "How can you say that when you don't know the exact time of death?"

"I know I'm not a killer."

The detective was cool, nearly nonchalant. "That remains to be seen. I do know something interesting."

Dexter snorted in disgust. "Please. Don't add to the suspense." His tone was sarcastic.

"Fred revised his will."

Phoebe bounced from her seat, hands clenched. "Who told you this?"

"His secretary. Apparently Fred wrote each of you a letter telling you so. He sent Bailey an invitation, presumably to give her the news in person. Why is that, Bailey? Why were you treated differently from the rest of your family?"

Bailey was clearly puzzled. "I have no idea."

Tyra glared at her cousin. "A simple phone call would have settled that matter, but then, we have to think about Uncle Fred. Simplicity wasn't his style." She swept her arm about the room. "Look at this place, a simple man wouldn't live in so lavish a place. The Painted Lady reeks of money. We all want it, even you, Bailey. We only have your word that Fred didn't tell you about the new will."

"You're so calm," Bailey said. "I didn't know about the will."

Anger flared in Tyra's voice. "Why pretend a grand love that wasn't there? Right now, shared blood isn't about sentiment, it's about money. I'm in line for a cut of Uncle Fred's estate. I don't care what his new will says. I want what's mine."

Sam forced himself to stay in his seat. "You people disgust me."

Tyra curled her top lip. "As if your opinion matters. After Hark releases us to go home, we'll never see one another again. Uncle Fred didn't want a formal funeral."

Bailey frowned. "How do you know?"

"He told me."

The detective cleared his throat. "Fred's lawyer confirms what Tyra says. Although I wasn't aware that the news was common knowledge."

Dexter poured Sybil a club soda. "It wasn't."

The detective spoke to the room. "Did anyone else know?"

There was no other confession of knowledge. To Tyra, the detective said, "You've moved up a notch on my short list."

Bailey turned to the detective. "So you've got your suspicions, I mean about who the most likely killer is?"

Before the detective could respond, Sybil did. "Don't we all have our suspicions?"

Bailey ignored her to speak to the detective. "Have you ruled out the hired help?"

"No."

"So no one is to trust anyone?" Tyra said.

Dexter laughed, the sound cynical and inappropriate for this serious occasion. "And then there were none."

Bailey recognized his words as the title of an Agatha Christie book. She realized from the laugh that Dexter truly did not care about what happened next. She needed time to think. "I'm gonna cook dinner."

Sam assessed her with understanding eyes. "I'll help you in the kitchen."

Sybil refused the club soda Dexter offered. "You two are ridiculous," she said to the Walkers. "So helpful. So cotton damn candy."

"But, Cousin Dearest," Dexter said to Sybil, "we do need to eat, and the cook is gone. If our little catering fanatic wants to make us dinner, let her.

I'm hungry and McDonald's isn't something I've got a taste for." Dexter turned to the detective. "Why is it that the cook is gone? You said everybody is a suspect."

"She wasn't here when the murder happened." He left out the rest, that if it was not for the fog, the people assembled in the parlor would not be there either, except for Sam and Bailey, the only suspects with a legitimate reason to be on-site.

Dexter said, "I think you've ruled out the cook and all the rest of the regular staff."

The detective said, "Correct."

Bailey said, "It's almost as if Uncle Fred wanted just the family to be present when he died. I mean, if his death turns out later to truly be suicide."

Sybil said, "That would suit his personality, but he couldn't have counted on the fog being dense enough to detain everyone indefinitely. I still say it's suicide. Maybe he planned to kill himself some other way on some other day but when we were stranded here by fog, he opted for the bathtub."

"No way," Dexter said.

The detective studied Dexter. "You're convinced Fred's death wasn't an accident?"

"Uncle Fred didn't have enough hair on his head for a blow-dryer. He has no wife or live-in girlfriend. There isn't anybody who stays here enough to warrant a blow-dryer, and even if there was, there'd be no reason for him to have it with him in the bathtub. I'm torn between thinking he did it and that one of us did."

Bailey said, "I'm thinking of John Grisham's book *The Testament*. In the book, a billionaire stages his own death after he changes his will. The new will punishes his close circle of relatives but rewards his distant relative, who is in fact his daughter, a long-lost and favored child."

Dexter's laugh ran beyond cynical to dangerous. "You can't possibly think you're his child."

"No," Bailey said, "but he did take the time to write me a personal invitation. That alone sets me apart from the rest of you."

Tyra said, "So?"

"So nothing," Bailey said. "The current scenario first reminded me of the Grisham book. Coincidentally, in the book, the motive for murder and for the changing of the will was money."

Dexter said, "Let me guess, the long-lost daughter in the Grisham book didn't want the money."

"Something like that," Bailey said. "I just want you guys to know that I'm no lost daughter, and I don't want Uncle Fred's money. I had no reason to kill him or to push him into killing himself."

The room was silent, each occupant ministering to his or her own thoughts.

Forty-eight hours ago, Bailey had been happy. She and Sam had enjoyed the forty-minute drive from New Hope to San Francisco, the fifteen-minute ride from the city limits to Fred's Dark Hill home.

To find themselves in a weird scene with her cousins and a detective who seemed anxious to solve a murder with more speed than accuracy was shocking and hard to believe, like a bad nightmare that had somehow gotten worse.

In the wake of Fred's demise, the officer in charge of the investigation held the Durham family in suspense with his subtle questions, each one purposefully drawing them deeper into zones of intense personal discomfort.

No one could move without close scrutiny, without wondering: Did she do it? Did he? Am I next? Those were the questions each cousin asked in private, that the detective asked in public, not with words but with his presence.

His presence represented the fact that even the impossible was possible, that goody-two-shoes Bailey was as big a suspect as Phoebe the former juvenile delinquent, as Tyra the compulsive gambler, as Dexter the gigolo, as Grant the charismatic, penniless serial entrepreneur.

For whatever reason, Fred Durham, aging business tycoon, had summoned this cast of characters together, one of whom the detective suspected was actually a murderer. Before he accused anyone of the crime, Hark Bittersweet needed proof, and in this case, probably a confession.

Bailey watched the detective as if she had the gift of mind reading. She faced him in the parlor, the setting elegant and authentically American Victorian in decoration and design. Polished oak formed the wainscoting, the mantel, and the window casings.

The cornices in the ceilings were of the same wood, the overall effect a sensual invitation to sit, relax, and enjoy the wealth so richly displayed in the home Fred Durham had adored as a man might adore the woman he loved.

Bailey found it hard to believe that normally peaceful people turned up dead by accident. For this reason, she was as suspicious about her uncle's death as the detective. The only person in the parlor she trusted was her husband, who, based on the detective's line of thinking, had as much to gain by Fred's death as Bailey. As her husband, Sam would benefit from any inheritance she gained.

Knowing this, Sam was defensive about the pointed police questioning even though it was expected and required by law and common decency. Sam watched as the detective opened his memo pad, found a clean page, and started scribbling notes without looking at anyone in particular.

The detective's action increased the tension in the parlor by a quick fifty percent. What was he writing? At last, the detective lifted his eyes from his scribbled notes, his gaze in direct opposition to Sam's.

Years of professional business etiquette came to Sam's rescue. He wanted to deck the detective. There had to be a better way to conduct this investigation than to corral everyone in the house together in a room that was growing smaller by the second. Sam felt claustrophobic, but losing his temper would accomplish nothing of value. He spoke to his wife. "Let's rummage up something for dinner."

Bailey warmed him with her eyes; filled with love, they soothed him. "Let's go."

The detective allowed them to leave the room, unconcerned they would escape the Painted Lady by way of the back door. There were policemen outside; no one would leave without Hark Bittersweet's permission.

Almost absentmindedly, the detective tapped the tip of his pencil on a scribbled page, closed the book, replaced it in his shirt pocket. Apparently he had been satisfied with his note-taking, although brief, but what had he written and why had he put the memo pad away?

A Hearty Dinner for the Harassed

Curried Chicken

Italian Green Beans

Scalloped Potatoes

Pineapple Torte

Iced Coffee

EIGHT

"Apparently," Sam said in the kitchen, "Fred wasn't so sweet after all."

Bailey gave him her full attention. "What do you mean?"

"He invited all these people together for dinner when he knew you guys didn't get along worth beans. I know we keep bringing this up, but it bothers me. I mean, what was the point?"

Bailey grimaced. "Maybe this situation really is a lot like the John Grisham story in which the victim set his relatives up to screw themselves over in their rush to get his money, only to find themselves more in debt and screwed up than ever before."

Sam's face was stern. "But why?"

"That's the multimillion-dollar question. I have no idea except maybe some twisted sort of revenge for people using him instead of loving him. Without more information, we're dealing with nothing but dead ends."

Bailey washed her hands and took stock of the kitchen supplies, aware she could make almost any dish she wanted. She started with the breast of chicken she found in the refrigerator. There was just enough for her to curry for dinner that night.

She lightly salted and peppered the chicken, put
the meat in a Corning Ware dish, and microwaved
it until it was done, the meat still moist and tender.

While the chicken cooked, she found a large
metal frying pan coated with Teflon. To the pan
she added real butter, which she melted on low.
To the butter she added chopped onion, garlic,
and bell pepper.

Once the vegetables were tender, she added
cream of celery soup and Pet milk. After the mixture had blended well, she added Worcestershire
sauce, fresh chopped ginger, curry powder, and
salt and pepper. She cubed the chicken on a cutting board and added the meat to the curry.

While the curry simmered, she prepared the
beans. She chose a medium-sized metal pot and
poured in three cans of green beans. She put
diced red peppers and onions in the beans, then
threw in a handful of commercially prepared ba-
con bits. Last, she poured a large can of crushed
tomatoes over the beans. She set the pot on a back
burner to let the beans bubble on medium until
the juice in the pot had boiled down.

While the beans bubbled, she assembled the potatoes Sam had peeled and thinly sliced. She prepared a basic white sauce, which she seasoned to
taste with Lawry's Seasoning Salt and standard
black pepper.

In a greased casserole, she alternated layering
the potatoes with a mozzarella-cheddar cheese
blend already shredded in a sealed bag she found
in the refrigerator, beginning and ending with the
potatoes.

She poured the thickened white sauce over the
mixture and sprinkled more cheese on top. She
baked the vegetables in the oven at 350 degrees

until the potatoes were tender. The smell coming from the oven was mouthwatering.

As the dinner simmered, bubbled, and baked, Bailey prepared the pineapple torte for a light dessert. The main ingredient she needed was a big can of crushed pineapple, which she found in the overstocked pantry.

While the pineapple drained, she made a crumb mixture of crushed vanilla wafers and melted butter. She pressed the cookie crumbs into a glass baking pan to form a crust along the bottom and sides of the pan.

In a medium-sized bowl, she creamed powdered sugar with butter. In a small bowl, she beat two large eggs, then poured them into the sugar mixture. Once the eggs, sugar, and butter were blended until smooth, she poured the mixture over the crushed cookie crust. On top of this, she spread the pineapple, which she topped with Cool Whip. She placed the dessert in the refrigerator to settle and cool.

Normally, Bailey would prepare the torte overnight, but these were not normal circumstances, and this was not a kitchen she was accustomed to using. It was her great fortune that her uncle had an excellent cook and a well-stocked kitchen because of it.

The act of cooking and sharing time with her husband had worked to soothe Bailey's jagged nerves. She said, "Sentiment aside, I think we've got a killer among us. I also think that if we don't figure out for ourselves what's going on around here, I'm afraid Detective Bittersweet will make his own conclusions about who did what and go on ahead with his retirement."

"I agree."

Bailey thought about Miss Marple, Agatha Christie's amateur detective in a collection of armchair cozy stories. Miss Marple used intuition, attention to very ordinary details, and personal insight to solve the mysteries in her own backyard.

Bailey pretended she was involved in her own armchair cozy. For three reasons, the setting was just right: (1) There was a mysterious death, (2) The suspects were marooned together, (3) The homicide detective was not clearly trusted in a place where no one felt safe.

"Sam," Bailey said, "I think we should start at the beginning."

"The invitation."

"Yes. I was so happy and surprised to get one. Except for the odd holiday card, I didn't keep up with Uncle Fred. I wouldn't know if he was in any sort of trouble or not, and I feel pretty bad about it now."

"Don't. Fred was active and social right until he was murdered. The invitation is a clue. Since he sent the invitation himself, he wanted you to be here. It's possible he suspected an attempt would be made on his life. The fact you received an invitation might mean he wanted you to be suspicious if he suddenly died, which he did."

"You're referring to the classic Durham family trait of being nosy, of course."

Sam nodded. "It was a long-standing joke between the two of you. In this case, use of the invitation was subtle, kind of like a red herring hidden away in a paragraph of a mystery novel."

Bailey laughed. "Talk about great minds thinking alike. I was just thinking of Miss Marple and pretending I'm her. You know, matronly, domesticated, ultraordinary, except for a surprise penchant for solving crimes."

"Which brings us to the killer," Sam said.

"Go on."

"I believe the killer wants to be caught."

"No way," Bailey said. "Anyone could have found Uncle Fred in the bathtub."

"All right, but the blow-dryer is as suspicious as the invitation. I think both are clues."

"Do you think that since Uncle Fred sent the invitation, he also dropped the blow-dryer into the tub?"

"It makes a weird sort of sense, but yes."

"Let's go with it for a minute," Bailey said. "If Uncle Fred did both of those things, he was being subtle in that he didn't openly commit suicide and crafty because he implicated a houseful of people in a suspicious death."

"Like you, Fred was a bookworm. Maybe he was counting on that common Durham trait, along with the nosiness to get to the bottom of whatever was bugging him before he died. Thinking along the lines of the Grisham book, let's figure Fred is the guilty one. That done, let's figure a reason for doing it. Electrocution is a nasty way to die."

Bailey started stacking dirty dishes. "In the Grisham book, the tycoon jumped out a window. Now, that was nasty."

"All the relatives were assembled at one location at the time the murder was committed."

"Suicide."

"Self-murder," Sam said. "Same thing."

Bailey leaned a hip against the center cooking island. "Okay, we're getting around to motive."

"Money."

"Right, it's the only thing Uncle Fred had that

kept the family together. He wasn't sentimental. Remember, we kept in touch by card during the holidays for the most part."

"That isn't true of everyone," Sam said. "The other relatives are local."

"And needy. We've never asked for anything."

"Like the invitation and the fact you discovered Fred's body, your relationship with Fred sets you apart from the rest of the family pack. We keep coming back to that, therefore it must be important."

"We don't know if any of this is correct, but it does feel as if Uncle Fred is talking to me from the grave. But you know what, Sam?"

"What?"

"There's more than money involved here."

"Such as?"

"The Painted Lady. She's part of Uncle Fred's wealth, but in a way, she stands out the same way I do. This house is about more than money, Sam. It's about family heritage. Tradition. It's Victoriana owned and passed down generation to generation by the same black family. The workmanship that went into this house is as unique as our family history. I've never cared about Uncle Fred's money, but I've always cared about this house."

"He knew it."

"But if he killed himself, he had to know the house probably would be sold."

"Which brings us again to motive. Fred's will. As a philanthropist, he could easily have left his estate to charity."

"I can't see that happening."

"But you agree it's possible," Sam said.

"Unfortunately, yes. As we both know, Uncle

Fred and I weren't close, but we had a good relationship."

"Unlike the rest of the Durham clan. I've never seen such avarice and misconduct in one family at the same time. No one is pulling together."

"If Uncle Fred killed himself, he would have anticipated the family's current reaction."

"True," Sam said. "That leaves Fred's goal, as in what he wanted to accomplish with his death."

"That is probably the million-dollar question," Hark Bittersweet said. He was dressed in his customary dark suit, and as usual, he looked relaxed and easygoing, his brand of camouflage.

Bailey eyed the detective with suspicion. "How long have you been eavesdropping?"

"I don't eavesdrop. I investigate."

Sam injected a note of threat in his voice. "Next time, announce yourself."

The detective sniffed the various pots and dishes. "It's been years since you were involved in a murder, but you've immediately put your sleuthing skills to use. Do you think it's wise to discuss your ideas in such an open area of the house? After all, anyone might be listening."

Bailey put her hands on her hips. "You don't act like a detective."

The detective maintained a bland expression. "You don't act like a typical grieving relative. You're approaching this . . . mystery in very analytical fashion. No tears. The fact you have the presence of mind to cook such a large meal is fascinating to me. Such objectivity in the middle of shocking disorder."

Sam folded his arms across his chest and glared. "You don't talk like a detective."

Hark Bittersweet gave Sam an I-don't-care-what-you-think look. "I talk like myself." As an after-thought he added, "Are you comparing me to Ridge Williams?"

Sam's voice was rough around the edges. "How do you know about Ridge?"

"It's my job to understand who I'm dealing with when I'm investigating a crime."

Sam eyed him coldly. "You said Fred was murdered. You were serious."

"Absolutely."

"I know about the missing fingerprints," Sam said, "but is there something else that makes you so positive?"

"The loose ends. Fred Durham was too meticulous a man to leave unanswered questions. Besides, there is no suicide note."

Bailey returned to her position against the counter. "There is the will, a long and legal document. Maybe he didn't leave a suicide note because he knew he had all his legal loose ends tied up."

"That could be true, but the biggest loose end of all is why Fred died."

Sam frowned. "Don't you mean, who killed Fred?"

"No. Once I find out why Fred died, I'll know who killed him."

Bailey sized up the detective. "You want our help to solve Fred's murder." This was not a question.

"I do. You two are the only people who seem to be thinking clearly, the only people openly thinking Fred's death wasn't an accident."

Sam spoke in a low, threatening tone. "What about my wife?"

"If she's innocent, the truth will clear her name.

If she's guilty, she's liable to trip herself up. The same goes for everyone."

"Including you."

It was the detective's turn to frown. "I don't follow."

Sam said, "I believe you do. You're quick to judge. As far as I'm concerned, you've got a conflict of interest going on with this . . . case. You're a family friend and a detective. If you know who the killer is and the two of you are in cahoots, then you could plant evidence that will convict an innocent person. I don't trust you."

"That makes us even."

Bailey said, "This is crazy. I'm standing here wanting to pinch myself. Uncle Fred was a generous old man who never hurt a living soul."

Hark Bittersweet eyed her impassively. "What makes you so sure?"

"My instinct."

"Aah," the detective said. "Woman's intuition. As you can guess, your intuition is worth squat at the moment. Facts are what's needed when the innocent need to be separated from the guilty. Fred might have been loving to you, but he wasn't loving to everybody else. He was ruthless when it came to making money."

Sam said, "We're back to motive."

"Precisely," the detective said. "The lack of money and the surplus of money. I suspect the killer lacked money and the victim had money to spare."

Bailey said, "You need to figure out who in the family was most in debt."

"Fine," the detective said. "Let's start with you."

Bailey said, "I've never borrowed money from Uncle Fred."

"How did you start your catering business?"

"Sam fronted the initial start-up costs. It's all documented."

Sam lowered his arms and balled his fists. "Be careful, Detective."

The detective inspected Sam's face. "Are you challenging me?"

"Take that statement any way you want."

"Considering a man has just died, I could take that statement quite seriously."

Sam inspected the detective right back. "Do that."

Bailey broke the visual wrestling match. "Detective, my husband and I understand you're conducting an official police investigation. We want to help."

The detective said, "I see this as an open-and-shut murder case. I expect to have the case completely solved within the week."

"That's when you retire," Sam said.

"Correct. I don't want any open cases. Fred Durham's murder is high profile."

Sam relaxed his fists but not his glare. "You need an ally, so you're enlisting our help."

"To save time."

A muscle flexed in Sam's jaw and neck. "I don't like you, Bittersweet."

"I'm after the truth."

Bailey figured she had better interrupt. "What if you don't have the truth before seven days are up?"

"I will."

Sam carried on as if Bailey had not spoken. "Your attitude does nothing to win my trust."

"Good. I don't trust you either, but you do have a proven track record for solving difficult and unexpected murder cases. You've got skills I can use right now."

Bailey's voice was hushed. "Is that legal?"

The detective looked outside the window. At that moment, the lights went out. In the dark, the detective laughed. He sounded genuinely amused. "Under these circumstances? Yes."

Bailey found her purse on the counter. She groped inside for emergency matches. She struck one. "What exactly do you want from us?"

"A profile on every person residing on the property at the time of the murder. Exclude from your list Fred's maid, his cook, and his gardener. I'll take care of them. You take care of the rest. After all, you're a Durham. The Durhams are known for their eccentricity. Who, besides Fred, could make millions building Victorian coaches for resort towns?"

When the lights came on again, the detective was gone.

Sam said, "I feel like I'm stranded on the island from hell and this house is the island. It's like all the elements worked together to create the perfect weirdo storm, a fog storm, power glitches included."

"It's true," Bailey said. "You can almost stab the air around here with a fork."

Sam pressed a kiss against her forehead. "We left home happy and looking forward to a great vacation. Today, we're trapped and looking at a mystery to solve. What a difference a day makes."

Bailey remembered something. *"Island of the Day Before."*

Sam closed the dishwasher and turned it on. "What?"

"There's an Italian writer named Umberto Eco

who wrote a book called *La isola del giorno primo,
The Island of the Day Before.*"

"Strange title."

"Catchy. Anyway, it's an imaginary island," Bailey
said. "In the story, no one can figure time in a
way that can be measured. Without time, the island
can't exist. It can only be viewed from a distance."

"So it was stuck on the day before?"

"Something like that," Bailey said. "Anyway, the
island isn't viewed the same way by everyone. Basically, you see what you want to see."

"Kind of like a reflection of someone's thoughts?"

"Yeah," Bailey said. "On the island, birds are
the color of jewels, foxes fly, and trees represent
signs of danger. I mean, what should have been
ordinary was anything but, like a dinner invitation
among family, people who should get along but
don't. Anyway, there's this special tree on the island called the Tree of Oblivion. It sits in the middle of everything. Anyone who eats fruit from this
tree finds perfect peace. I keep thinking that somewhere in this house is one thing that will explain
away everything."

"A note from Fred," Sam said.

"I suppose so. Do you think the new will was
simply a lie, that Uncle Fred told the rest of the
family he had cut them out of his will, only he
really hadn't? Do you think this could have been
some sort of sick joke on his part?"

"It's possible."

Bailey's brain was on overload. The day before
her arrival on Dark Hill she had been bored but
at peace. At the center of that peace had been her
marriage. Her marriage, like Umberto Eco's island,
was not pictured the same way by everyone who
witnessed it.

Fern and Sage viewed their marriage with the eyes of innocence. Sam and Bailey viewed their marriage from two perspectives: his and hers. At the center of their marriage were their wedding vows, and those vows were their tree of oblivion, their anchor in the middle of life's uncertainties, their strength, an energy Bailey drew on now. The look she shared with Sam implied he felt the same way she did.

He said, "I think Bittersweet is right about one thing, we'll need a confession, either from one of your relatives or from a suicide note. Fred's death is strange but otherwise perfect as far as murder goes. He or his killer could have dropped the blow-dryer in the tub with his bath cloth to avoid fingerprints."

"*Island of the Day Before,*" Bailey said.

"Right," Sam said. "Point of view depends on perspective. We should pick one: Either assume he did it or assume someone else did it and try to prove it. We'll keep going around in circles if we don't do that. Concentrating on one thing will keep us from feeling overwhelmed."

"Yeah. This situation reminds me of what happened when Mary Lou Booker was thrown overboard on a cruise ship on her wedding anniversary. Her death was so simple, her murderer almost got away with the crime. But you think Fred really did do it to himself?"

"It's the angle I'd like to work," Sam said. "All I know is that we need a plan."

"Like what?"

"Keep an eye on Bittersweet by working with him. Develop a time line for each person."

"I get it, Sherlock, by proving each person was

alone when Fred died, we'll prove that only Fred could have killed himself."

"You've got it, Watson."

Bailey grinned. "Let's do it."

A Snack for the Snoops

One crystal bowl of bite-sized Tostitos brand
tortilla chips

One matching cup of mild El Paseo salsa

Two liters of 7-Up

NINE

Sunday afternoon

Sam and Bailey were in the parlor. Bailey sat across from her cousin Dexter who declined her offer of chips and salsa. He said, "You've got a whole lot of nerve, cuz."

Like Dexter, Bailey preferred not to mince words. "So do you."

Dexter's laugh was short and bitter. "I don't have to answer any of your questions," he said. "You're not a cop. I don't care how many crimes you helped solve. The fact that you were involved in a murder at all isn't natural."

"I agree this is a weird situation, but I am family. Maybe you know something about Uncle Fred you'd feel better telling me instead of Hark Bittersweet."

Dexter wore an incredulous look on his face. "I know Hark a whole lot better than I know you."

"We're blood."

"We aren't close, Bailey. Cut the crap."

"Okay, you're so tense. I can't help but wonder why. I think you're paranoid about something."

Dexter visibly forced himself to relax. "Who

wouldn't be? I don't even know if it's legal for Hark to keep us together in this house."

"We're all staying because we want to stay. It's like a soap opera, nobody wants to miss a scene."

"You scare me, Bailey."

Her grin was wily. "I'll take that as a compliment."

"Arrogant too."

"Confident. There's a difference."

The cousins faced each other. Like two gunfighters on a deserted street in the middle of a western town, each did not trust the other not to shoot too soon. Dexter was fidgety. His foot beat a rapid tattoo against the floor.

Bailey's laugh was genuine. "If you're trying to look calm, Dexter, you're failing."

"You can't toy with me like a cat plays with a mouse she plans to eat for dinner. You're not a professional, and I'm not a killer."

"You're a playboy."

"What I am is none of your business," Dexter said. "I seriously doubt we'll even see each other again when all this craziness blows over. After all, the world keeps spinning. We'll all get old and gray and wind up dead eventually. It was Fred's time to die and so he did."

Bailey was appalled. "You callous bastard."

"Honest bastard. Get it straight."

"How do you earn your money, you honest bastard?"

Dexter glanced at Sam, who was silent as a hole in the wall, then returned his gaze to Bailey. "I usually escort women to various functions in the city. This means I show up in my leased Mercedes and step into the persona of the perfect date. I don't have a set of offices anywhere or any specific place of business."

"You're a gigolo."

"Escort. Playboy. Not a gigolo."

Bailey tried to keep the censure she felt off her face. She failed. "Do you prostitute yourself for money?"

If Dexter was offended by her question, he chose not to show it in his face or his body language. "Low blow, cuz. There are a lot of single women in the business world who don't have a steady man. They don't want strings any more than I do. I like the way I make my living. I don't hurt anyone, and I fill a niche, so to speak."

Bailey scanned him with her pretty brown eyes. "So you pick women up and take them wherever they want to go. What about after?"

Dexter shrugged his shoulders and recrossed his legs at the knee. "There is no after. I take money up front and then I do whatever the woman wants me to do as long as it's legal."

"Including sex."

"Excluding sex, unless it's off the clock. I've got two scruples, Bailey. One, I don't sell the use of my family jewels and two, I don't kiss and tell. Unless I'm seen in public with someone, I don't discuss the women I date. It's the key to my success, that and old-fashioned good service."

"Okay, do you have special days of the week when you do this?"

"Weekends only. I include Thursday as part of the weekend. Monday, Tuesday, and Wednesday are my personal days."

"You keep a calendar?"

"Of course."

"Honest, meticulous bastard," Bailey said.

Dexter grinned recklessly, but his eyes were cold. "In that order."

"Was someone blackmailing you?"

"No."

"Did you borrow money from Uncle Fred?"

"No."

"Why did he invite you to dinner?"

"Same reason he invited you. He wanted to see me."

"You're lying," Bailey said.

"Maybe."

"I'll find out."

"Unless I killed Fred, which I didn't, whether I'm lying or not right now is irrelevant. The man is dead. I didn't do it. Interrogate somebody else." He paused to study her insolently. "Cuz."

Bailey had to fight to control her temper. She thought Dexter was cold, but if what he said was true, he did have standards and, surprisingly, she believed him when he said he did not kill Fred. She believed him because Fred's death had been a messy business.

The killer had to enter Fred's bathroom, a very private place. Fred was naked, which was extremely intimate. She did not think Dexter would put himself in that type of situation.

If Dexter killed someone, Bailey figured he would do it from a distance: He might hire a hit man, someone else to do the physical work, and act as a buffer between himself and the crime. No, she did not believe Dexter was the killer, but she believed he knew something important he was not telling her.

She said, "Withholding evidence in a criminal investigation is illegal."

"And your point?"

"I want to know what was in his new will, if in fact he really did have a new will. Fred's lawyer was pretty closemouthed on the subject," Bailey said.

"Look," Dexter said, "why should I jeopardize my own safety by screwing around with Uncle Fred when it came to the will? No, thank you, but I will say this: Fred was a philanthropist on the one hand, extremely private on the other. Underneath all that, he was a shrewd businessman."

"He'd have to be shrewd to turn the Painted Lady into a showpiece instead of the white elephant it could have been. It takes money to live on Dark Hill."

"That's not what I'm driving at, Bailey."

"Okay, could you be more specific?"

"It wouldn't surprise me if Fred staged his own death. I think he wanted something. I think that whatever it was he wanted could only be achieved by his dying."

"His will."

"Yes."

Bailey rested her back against the sofa, legs crossed, body still. She looked puzzled but determined. "I suppose none of us needs an excuse to be here because we're all relatives. Because we're all relatives we each have something substantial to gain, which brings us not to the will but to Fred's business sense."

Dexter whistled softly. "I wondered when you would get around to taking your emotions out of the problem. For a . . . what is the politically correct term to use? . . . stay-at-home mom, you're pretty savvy."

"Don't try to shift the subject from Fred's money to my personal lifestyle."

"That's my point, Bailey. I can't shift your mind at all. But consider this, you're as guilty as the rest of us for not being closer to Fred. If he was having money trouble or if he worried his life was in danger, he didn't confide in you either."

"He said he wanted to talk to me."

"Did he?"

"No."

Dexter's eyes on Bailey were cold. "So, you're suggesting he was killed by someone in this house to keep him from talking to you about . . . what?"

"I think Uncle Fred wanted me here to stand up for him after he died."

"Assuming he knew he'd die."

Bailey ignored the sarcasm. "This coming together he wanted was a reunion of the family. That means something."

"Probably," Dexter said. "I wonder how Hark Bittersweet feels about you harassing the, uh, suspects."

"Asking questions isn't hurting his investigation."

"Asking questions is hurting your position within the family. What you're doing has drawn a line between you and the rest of us, Bailey."

"I'm not the enemy here."

This time, Dexter allowed his anger to show. His face was flushed, his eyes hard. "You're like a bad blister on everybody's neck."

Sam put down his glass of 7-Up. He dusted the salt of the tortilla chips off his hands. He left his corner of the room, his movements unhurried, lithe, the look in his eyes lethal, perhaps even feral.

His wife was the focal point of their amateur investigation, the speaker, but he was the observer, the one with the global view of the problem they faced together. In this global view, there was no room for emotion, for sentiment: Sam would do anything to protect his wife, anything at all, including murder.

While Bailey ran her mouth, challenging everyone, while she stirred and cooked in other people's pots, Sam was the true hero of the drama they all shared, not Bailey, not Detective Bittersweet. Sam's only interest in the Durham clan was his wife. In this regard, he never wavered, he never second-guessed, he never took chances, ever.

Wanting to keep his skin intact, Dexter stood. On his way out of the parlor, he made a final parting shot. "Bailey?"

"Yeah?"

Dexter's smile was slight and crooked with irony. "You've got the one thing Fred didn't have."

"What?"

"Sam."

TEN

It was Monday, the day of the funeral. Bailey and Sam stood alone, everyone else several feet away as Fred's ashes were scattered to the wind and to the bay he loved. The fog was present, as oppressive as rain, and Sam used a borrowed umbrella to cover his wife's head from the dampness in the air.

Her grief was silent, as was his own, as they shared their makeshift shelter from the moist air, which clung to their exposed skin, like dew. It was cold, it was wet, but thankfully, there was no wind to chill them to the bone.

Even though it was late June in San Francisco, the temperature so close to the water of the bay was always cooler than in cities like New Hope or San Jose, cities nestled firmly in a valley whose hills were scored with oak, olive, and eucalyptus trees.

Bailey was mainly aware of Sam, her relatives relegated to the fringe of her conscious mind. Her thoughts were all turned inward, her feelings numb with suppressed grief. Her sense of loss in those final rites of Fred Durham's life were on hold, at least until the truth about why he died was bared to them all.

Until the truth was fully known, there could be

no real justice, no true way to mourn in peace. The circumstances of Fred's death were a specter of controversy, a living ghost between the surviving relatives, those who wanted the case closed and those who wanted the case to stay open.

When it was over, when all the truths were made public, Bailey vowed that she and Sam would continue their life's journey, they would travel along the California coastline and marvel at its untamable spirit, they would go home to New Hope and to the family they had created together, and their daughters would be ready for them, waiting for them, prepared to love them once more in that unconditional way that children love and honor their mother and father, regardless of how good or bad they are as caregivers.

Bailey's mind cried the word *no,* over and over. Those could not be her uncle's ashes. Among his assembled mourners could not be a killer, but then Sam, ever watchful, ever in tune with her deepest self, sensed the inner upheaval threatening to rip the word *no* from her mind, from her mouth.

Sam tossed propriety and the umbrella to the ground and pulled her to rest beneath the shelter of his coat, where she pressed her body against the heat of his chest. A true northern California native and seasoned traveler, Sam had known it was wise to bring coats and sweaters along for their two-week trip.

He knew the sun could be shining in New Hope and obscured by the fog along the coastal towns where he and his wife would be traveling. He was thankful for his foresight, thankful he was big and strong enough to shield his trembling woman from the speculative view of those present, those people who would connive against her.

Fred had loved Bailey, but only from a distance. Sam loved her in every sense there was for a man to love a woman, in mind, in spirit, and in flesh. His was a carnal knowledge, brutal in the hard path it cut from his heart to his soul.

Yes, Sam used his heavy build to shield her grief from the vultures that were her relatives, and in the process he gave to her his strength, his will to continue to fight the good fight, the kind of fight in which truth and justice always prevailed.

And then, Bailey lifted her eyes, her chin to meet the challenge he silently posed to her to gather her wits about her and begin, again, to chisel away at the evil root that fed the greed in her family tree.

These were strangers, her relatives—Phoebe, Tyra, Sybil, Grant, and Dexter Durham—people who never had the profound bond of childhood secrets between them, who never knew the pride of shared accomplishments as adults.

Theirs was a generation of small-minded, self-centered, avaricious, gold-digging blood kin, and yet Bailey was different from all the rest, so different that she had stepped away from her twisted roots to form a new life with the Walker family, and she had been rewarded for her steadfast application of all the good things that made living worthwhile: great food, fine friends, and the respect of the community in which she lived and worked.

Bailey threw back her shoulders, her determination at once focused and renewed. As if on cue, the assembled mourners broke free of the trance the scattering of Fred's ashes had imposed upon them all.

As if they were a collection of raven-winged

birds, they moved on one accord, they returned to
their cars and their private thoughts. They headed
off to turn the corner they all had to turn together, the corner in life that left each one of
them orphans in a sense because there was no
elder Durham among them, no mentor, no link to
a past they had all taken for granted, including
Bailey, a past heavily intertwined with the Old
West, the frontier John Durham had conquered as
a former slave and self-made man of fortune.

Inside Sam's sleek black sedan, Bailey kept her
chin high, and resolved to never again take Sam
for granted. He was the man she most admired in
the world, the man who was more than the spice
in her life, more than the man who listened to
her dreams and to her fears, he was her anchor,
the best friend she ever had, a gift of being that
money could not buy, ever, something Fred Durham, because of his jaded, manipulative personality
and his multimillion-dollar bank account, had
never hoped to possess. It was this, more than the
spreading of Fred's ashes, that pushed Bailey's determination to get the whole ugly truth out into
the bitter open, into high gear.

Sam drove on, not overly worried about the future; rather, he was focused on the present, the
sound of his wife's breathing, the lift of his wife's
chin, the squaring of her shoulders, the heat of
their rekindled love.

Three hours after Fred's last rites, Bailey's mind
turned again to the strangeness of the day, to the
way Fred's wishes had been carried out to the letter, as expressed to the family through his lifelong
attorney and advisor, Malinder Simmons.

The fog had thinned, and even though a veil
remained, it was still beautiful in San Francisco.

The Walkers still had a view of the city and of the bay, a view that would have—had it not been for the thickness in the air—appeared limitless.

Standing in the parlor window with Bailey, all the rest of the relatives residing either in their own homes or in private suites within the Painted Lady, Sam spoke to his wife. "You okay?"

"As much as I can be. It just seems weird, Sam, that Uncle Fred died and the world kept on going as if nothing happened."

"It only makes the truth sweeter, Bailey."

The skin beneath her eye twitched in denial. "What do you mean?"

"Honor makes the difference. Truth makes the difference. Love makes the search for honor and truth worthwhile. The way I see it, Bailey, you're the only member of your family who really cared about Fred the man and not Fred the millionaire. You make the difference by keeping Fred's corner of the world from forgetting he existed. Your being here, in the Painted Lady, the place Fred loved more than anything, is special, significant because he made a point to invite you here, probably knowing death was imminent."

Bailey rested her cheek against her husband's chest, the sound of his heart sturdy and steady in her ear. "If that's true, then you're the reason I'm able to keep going in the middle of all this . . . heartache. I feel like a thorn in everybody's side, Sam. If I wasn't here, I think my cousins would be dividing the furniture and hauling it off by now, right down to the antique doorknobs."

Bailey had begun to hate her part in the resolution of Fred's drama. She wanted to fade into the background, to be a spectator instead of an investigator. She wanted Hark Bittersweet to do his job and leave the details to his official support staff, but the truth would never be discovered from the outside looking in, never, and because Bailey knew this, she shook off her misgivings about the role she played in Fred's drama.

Responsibility was always about doing the right thing, not the comfort thing, or even the respectable thing. It was about facing consequences, about being just, being fair, no matter who was hurt in the process.

Sam continued to inspect the dying embers of the Durham family fire, flames ignited by Fred's electrocution, and stoked by the idea of murder. There were embers glowing hot in the Painted Lady, hot and ready to burn even the house down.

With his eyes, Sam flicked through the cast of characters before him and was amazed, yet again, that Bailey turned out to be normal, with a healthy woman's gift of loving and giving. Yes, he was lucky to call her his own, damn lucky, and he knew it.

Sam shrugged his tense shoulders to loosen them. "From what I've seen, that might very well be true. Like I said, your being here is significant."

"This whole business is depressing: talk of a changed will that cuts everyone out except me, talk of murder versus suicide, the idea Detective Bittersweet is rushing the investigation in order to retire on a high note in his career."

These days would always stand out in Bailey's mind, always. Sam had kept his temper under control, even though it raged through him in waves of heat that touched the cold spot in Bailey's heart that had been with her since the discovery of her uncle's body.

While it was true that Sam had remained civil throughout all the shenanigans, Bailey sensed he

SACRED LOVE 115

could easily slip over the edge of his control. He was angry at the proceedings, but he was stout enough in spirit not to allow his temper to side-track him off his quest for justice. There were looks he gave to her alone, as if he willed her to believe in him, his ability to keep her safe. And she did believe in him, her best friend.

Hers was a hero who truly existed, not as a fig-ment of her imagination, but as a flesh-and-blood man. Even though their immediate future was un-easy, Bailey's love for Sam was only strengthened by the emergency they faced, and when she thought hard and true about it, she realized that her love for him would remain the way it had al-ways been, intact and unchanged; but, Bailey was frightened, for herself and for Sam.

"There's a lot going on emotionally," he said after a while. "I can't help you with that. As callous as it sounds, I just don't have the same connection to your family that you do."

Bailey wrapped her arms around his waist, squeezing him tight. At his best, Sam appreciated her open mind and her willingness to get to the bottom of a problem, even when the going was rough. "Your being here is enough," she said.

"My being here is all about your protection. Somebody in this house is guilty of murder, and everybody in this house is guilty of at least cruelty, including us."

"No."

"Yes," Sam said. "We aren't crying and gnashing our teeth because Fred's dead. Part of that is be-cause he'd already lived a long life and enjoyed it thoroughly while he lived it. Instead of going home to mourn, we're disengaging our feelings to the point where we see and judge everybody the same: as a suspect, including Detective Bittersweet."

"If I didn't know you better," Bailey said, "I'd say you have a heart of stone, or ice in your veins. One of those clichés."

"Now is no time to be beat around the bush, and I'm not going to, no matter whose toes I crush. The Durhams are supposed to be a family, but you treat one another like enemies, an attitude I don't need to understand, just accept the way it is."

"You're right about that," Bailey said. "Whatever went wrong with this family, it's too late to fix now."

"Regardless," Sam said, "I want Fred's death investigated and closed but not at your expense. To this end, I'm dealing with people at face value."

"Let's go home."

When she tried to pull free from his arms, Sam refused to release her. "No, Bailey. It's too late."

His arms around her were hard, the knotted muscles pressing tight against her body as tough as his decision to stand his ground. Bailey trembled, not from fear Sam would actually hurt her, but from fatigue. "Why?"

Sam's eyes were cold, dark, ominous. "Your relatives can knock on our door any time. This means we can inadvertently let a killer into our house. No. This mess started here, on Dark Hill. It ends here."

An oppressive sorrow weighed heavy in Bailey's voice, in Bailey's heart. There were times when Sam couldn't care less what other people around him thought of his survival tactics when dealing with difficult people, and this was one of those times. Even though she knew Sam was right to be on guard, Bailey just wished everyone could get along. "So we keep on not trusting anybody."

Sam rubbed his open palm through her hair, the strands of it feeling warm, thick, curly to his touch. "Family life isn't always apple pie, sweetheart, and you know it. People have killed for money or greed or passion inside the same family long before this happened to Fred, and if that's the case here, we'll deal with it and move on."

Bailey sighed as if her very soul were both ancient and tired, as if she might lay her head down and cry. If she did, she knew that her husband would be there to console her. She also knew he would do nothing differently when it came to dealing with her relatives. "You make it sound so simple."

"It is."

She studied the look in his eyes until she read the only truth in his mind that made sense of his attitude, which was almost brutal and entirely singleminded. The last time Sam had been this hard-nosed it had been during their investigation of a murdered boy's death at the hands of a skinhead gang, a group of society's misfits. "Maybe it is, if you take all the emotion out of it."

Sam held nothing back. "Which is precisely what I've done and there is no need for me to apologize, not when it comes to protecting you. I was a good man to start with, Bailey, but you made me the man I am now."

"I wish I could believe that, but you're too committed and too determined to be anything other than the kind of man you are: solid, comforting, full of integrity."

He laughed. "Not sexy?"

Bailey laughed, too, even though she was totally

serious. Sam was a high achiever who seldom thought in terms of defeat. The sticky problems posed by Fred Durham's death had him fired up. "Very sexy, but it's not the glue that keeps me by your side night after night. It's not even love."

"What is it?"

Her response was quick. "The integrity."

"Oh, yeah?"

"Yeah," Bailey said, as she cited the buttons he pushed for her. "You do what you say you're gonna do. You understand that being a good husband goes beyond fidelity and coming home sober every night. You know it's more than paying bills on time and all the normal, expected things that go on inside a marriage."

His tone was teasing. "You're making me blush."

"Stop kidding, Sam."

He kissed her forehead, then brushed her cheek with his fingertips when he was done. "I'm not kidding. I'm human, sweetheart. Don't make me out to be more than I am. If you aren't disappointed now, someday you will be."

She pressed her fingers against his lips. His lips felt full, pliant, and warm, the words coming from them so jaded. "Don't say that."

He kissed her slender fingers, one by one. "A day will come when the distractions of raising children and establishing ourselves will be over. When that happens, Bailey, it'll just be me and you again. When you look at me then, you'll see just how human, just how ordinary I am."

It was her turn to smile, a look so starkly radiant that it warmed her husband from the inside out. Sam might be rude to anyone he felt was a potential troublemaker in their lives, but he was seldom rude to her. "Never," she said. "When I have the blues, you know what to do to chase them away, whether it's taking me dancing or out to dinner or watching an old Bette Davis movie with me while I pig out on brownies or chocolate cake."

He laughed, this time from the belly.

For a man who rarely practiced self-deception, Sam tended to have a rose-colored view of his own wife. There were times when Bailey was glad to bask in the glow of that beautifully colored light, and other times, like now, when she wanted him to see her clearly and to take her seriously, in her own time and in her own way, not just when it suited him to lend her his ear. "You understand that when I want to be alone some days, it's not a rejection of you, but a rejuvenation of the spirit for me."

"You sound like a women's magazine."

Disgusted, she gave up. One thing Bailey had learned early in their marriage was that her husband had a huge case of tunnel vision when he chose to keep his mind narrow and his thoughts on easy street. "Don't go sexist on me, Sam."

"I'm serious. I'm a man like any other man. I make mistakes, learn from them, and go on. I love my wife and kids and take care of them the best way I can, but I can also do wrong. Why? I'm not perfect. I don't want your worship. I just want your love."

Her arms fell away from his waist. She took one step back, her face turned up to his. She read mixed signals in his demeanor. Sam was a doer, the kind of man who moved from one activity to another without losing control or momentum.

To be stuck in the Painted Lady, to be conscious of every step he took at Bailey's side, was driving him crazy. Sam was so afraid he might miss a clue that he had a hard time reining in his energy.

He wanted to be pounding on doors and maybe a few faces to get the answers he wanted about the mysterious events taking place on Dark Hill. Sam was being patient, not in a peaceful sense but more in the manner of an animal lying in wait for its supper. "You're trying to tell me something. What is it?"

"I will kill for you, Bailey. Right here, right now. My biggest fear is that I don't think you're going to get away from this mess without a scratch. Based on the animosity I've seen, it wouldn't shock me if somebody else is killed or injured before this day is done. The way I see it, somebody in this house has nothing to lose. I do. I won't lose you, not over somebody else's greed."

"And you tell me not to think you're a god."

"I didn't say that," Sam said.

"Not exactly, but you did when you reminded me you're human. If I don't walk out of the Painted Lady alive, it'll be because it's my time to die."

Sam pressed her body to his chest, hard. His voice was rough, savage in its intensity. "Don't say that."

"I'm only saying what you're thinking. I've lived with you for twenty years, Sam. I may not know all your secrets but I do know the way you think. You think that if you keep me separated from the girls, you can focus all your attention on my survival, but what about your survival, Superman? What makes you think I won't kill for you?"

Abruptly, he shoved her away. "I don't wanna to talk about this."

"I hate it when you get macho."

Trying hard to suppress the wild, territorial way he felt, Sam forced his voice into a casual tone. He felt anything but casual. "I thought I was sensitive."

Bailey rolled her eyes. "This is serious. Yes, you're the man, and yes, you'll do everything in your power to keep me safe, but it works both ways. We're both at risk here and neither one of us wants this mess to follow us home. Don't second-guess me and don't patronize me."

She was right, but Sam chose not to admit it. Still using a casual tone, he said, "I've got integrity, remember?"

Bailey had too much experience with Sam to be fooled by his present attitude. She knew quite well he was trying to lull her into a more docile and pliable mood, his goal to distract her from talk about placing his safety above her own.

"As you said, you're also human. So am I. We need to do what we do best and that's work together. It's the way we've solved cases before. Uncle Fred's death is emotional for me—and you—but if we change what we do best, which is to watch each other's back, we set ourselves at odds with each other. If we do that, we both lose."

"Brains and beauty, too." Lowering his head, Sam leaned down to kiss her; only just as their lips met, a man behind them cleared his throat. It was Detective Bittersweet.

ELEVEN

Quiet, yet observant, Detective Bittersweet had eased into the Durham family background while Fred Durham was being laid to rest. With all the controversy going on about the method and timing of Fred's death, there was little attention to the fact that Hark shared a history with the deceased.

Because of his old family ties, as close or perhaps closer than Fred's blood relatives, Hark also stood to inherit a sizable piece of the Durham estate—at least he had been in line to inherit prior to the change in Fred's will, which had yet to be read by attorney Malinder Simmons.

It was Hark who served as liaison between Fred and many of the community projects Fred had supported as a local philanthropist. Fred gave money for after-school programs, supplies and materials for several neighborhood gardens run by school-children, ages twelve through eighteen.

In Fred's opinion, children were more than keys to the future, they were the future. For Fred, if there were no children, there could be no true forgiveness among men, no chance for long-term justice, no real way to keep evolving from the brutal beginnings that inspired a former slave, John

Durham, to dig his way up from the bowels of civil poverty: the ownership of one man by another.

Once Tiger Woods hit the golfing scene, once sisters Venus and Serena Williams began their domination of tennis courts around the world, Fred Durham provided seed money and materials for after-school golf and tennis programs. He believed that athletes opened doors between cultures, that young athletes knocked down doors, and poor athletes needed money, of which he had plenty to spare.

In life, it had been Fred's policy to reward excellence with time when he had it, with money when he did not, both methods his way of reminding himself of his family's humble beginnings, as slaves, as miners, as risk-taking entrepreneurs.

In the entrepreneurial spirit, Fred was respected in the Dark Hill community as a good man with a tremendous heart; it was the reason his death had remained in the newspapers every day since it happened, why reporters hung around the mansion and the police station searching for gossip about the Durham family.

All the side action kept the fire burning on Hark's determination to solve Fred's murder before he retired in less than a week. He felt it was a fitting way to honor the man who treated him like the son he never had, a child he could train in the art of carriage making and financial empire building. Hark did not miss Fred's money, but he did miss Fred's smile, his oddball sense of humor, his dapper style.

As Hark watched, Sam shoved Bailey behind his back as if he was ready to brawl right there in the parlor. The detective assessed the younger man's mood accurately: Sam was pissed at being caught off guard in a quiet moment with his beautiful wife. To diffuse the volatile situation, Hark was the first to speak. "Sorry to interrupt."

Bailey eased from behind her husband's back to stand at his side. She extended her hand to the detective. "No problem," she said.

Sam said nothing.

Bailey squared her shoulders. She looked elegant and genteel standing next to her husband. She noticed that the detective's smile was winning, but it stopped short of his eyes. His eyes told a strange story of their own. What story? Bailey wondered. What story would they tell if she and Sam were to discover he was the killer among them? "What do you want?" she asked.

"Answers."

Sam took one step forward, a muscle flexing in his jaw, his expression stripped clean of all thought, all emotion. "Careful, Detective."

"To get answers," said the detective, "I need to think of the right questions. Like you, I returned to the Painted Lady so I won't miss any . . . action. Like you, I came into the parlor to unwind for a minute. I've been in this room many times as a guest of Fred's. I half expect him to walk through the door any minute. I miss him."

"Want a drink?" Bailey asked. "I know it's ordinary to have food and a reception after a funeral, but nothing like that was done here. My uncle's orders per Malinder Simmons."

"I couldn't eat anyway," the detective said. "I'll get a drink for myself."

The Walkers moved to a corner of the parlor designated for intimate conversation. There were two overstuffed chairs, a small round table with a Tiffany lamp on top, and a view of the street below. Speaking strictly to each other—about what, the detective was unable to hear—the couple proceeded to ignore him.

Brandy in hand, standing at an opposite window, a small courtyard its primary view, the detective slid his gaze over Sam and was thankful they were operating on the same side of the law; he was convinced of that now—Sam was as suspicious as ever.

Sam's reaction to his surprise visit to the Painted Lady, so soon after Fred's ashes were scattered, confirmed Hark's hunch that the Walkers were innocent of any wrongdoing, a hunch that hit him during the administering of Fred's final rights.

It was apparent to the detective that Fred's relationship with Bailey had functioned within some type of neutral zone, a place where they both shared the benefit of familial pride, kinship, and even love. Of all the immediate family, it was increasingly clear that Bailey was the most stable.

From the police reports his team had gathered and from his own observations, the detective believed Bailey's value system most closely resembled Fred's than that of any other surviving member of Fred's family.

It took very little digging on the part of Hark's office staff to discover that Bailey worked beside her husband to provide time and leadership to the New Hope community they had lived in for the major portion of their marriage, a community nearly as old and respected as Fred's own Dark Hill.

With Fred's money and business connections, the Walkers would have the power to better influence the lives and destinies of another generation of school-age children, which in turn would continue the positive part of the Durham legacy.

The more the detective thought about it, based on his personal association with Fred, the more Fred's new will, if it existed, made sense: The Walkers could work along the same philanthropic lines Fred used in his own Dark Hill neighborhood and surrounding communities. In this way, Fred's good works would continue.

In turn, Sam and Bailey would gain more than money, more than corporate power, they would gain a truly refined, uplifting sense of their own giving spirits, hallmarks of the natural philanthropist each of them was in his and her own right; in this way, the detective mused, the Walkers were perfectly matched, with themselves as a couple and beyond themselves because of Fred's ambition.

Fred, with his on-target business savvy, his knack for hiring just the right people for just the right job, a secret to his continued financial success, would have known this about them, he would have found a way to ensure the Walkers would benefit, not from his death, but from his life's work.

True, the detective reasoned, Bailey would have a motive for murder—money—but based on her family life, her marital stability, and her penchant for solving crime, he never once truly considered her a serious suspect in Fred's death.

Fred's death had moved from the emotional to the clinical to the technical in Hark Bittersweet's mind. Once the shock of Fred's death was over, it had been easier for the detective, like Sam, to step back emotionally from what had happened. After all, homicide, in all its forms, was the detective's field of expertise.

The medical examiner's report provided all the clinical information needed, and now it was up to Hark to lay out the technical aspects of the crime:

the who, the what, and the why of murder. He already had the when and the where answered during the emotional phase; when: the night of the dinner party; where: the master suite.

So far, no matter how brutal and direct Hark treated the Durham relatives in his private conversations with them, they continued to move forward as if the current family drama was more an inconvenience than a devastating event of catastrophic proportions.

For all the deep concern the family displayed, Hark was hard pressed to figure any one of them felt enough passion to kill Fred, especially in the up-close and intimate way it was done, in the bathtub, a method that was downright malicious, and not easy to do considering the personal chemistry that would exist between a victim and killer from the same family.

The word *malicious* made the detective think of hatred, a passion. Passion was hot. The cold counterpoint to this hot passion was greed. Within the parameters of the family setting, the greed was universal, a common denominator; however, the malicious nature of the crime was not. He felt as if the investigation was going round and round, and like a dog chasing his own tail, he was getting nowhere. Yet, Hark believed that pursuing one particular angle of the investigation, motive in the form of hatred, would unlock the mystery of Fred's death.

Hark's goal upon entering the parlor had been to figure out his next step: how to select the most spiteful person in a group of spiteful individuals; his answer: one question at a time, one observation at a time, until he resolved what was nearly a perfect crime.

From his chair beside Bailey, who was talking nonstop about the funeral, the relatives, a possible conspiracy theory between her cousins, Sam lifted his glass of Perrier to the detective in a silent warning to tread lightly: He had not been oblivious to the detective, he had been watching him all along.

Bailey had also been thinking, an apprehensive attitude growing inside her as a result of it. She had felt the same way when her friend Mary Lou Booker died in the first suspicious death she and Sam had investigated.

At that time, Bailey was suspicious of Mary Lou's husband, Hurley, a prominent man who should have been above suspicion of murder but was not. What she learned from that experience was to trust her heart as much as she trusted her eyes, something she was able to do best with Sam by her side.

Sam's presence kept her fear at bay. Having him around meant she could be as nosy as she wanted without worrying too hard someone might knock her lights out for getting too close to whatever truth there was for her to discover.

Bailey could not stop thinking about the scattering of Fred's ashes or the idea that those ashes were all that remained of a hero to so many charities and children's organizations. It disturbed her that on every emotional level her cousins did not appear to take Hark Bittersweet too seriously; none of them showed fear in the face of his official police role. When the detective was present, they hardly treated him any different than they treated one another.

There should have been discomfort in the knowledge that Hark was paying close attention to every spoken word, every facial expression, every body movement. Even though Bailey had nothing to hide, she felt uneasy knowing her entire life was under microscopic study.

Were her cousins so relaxed with the detective because they knew he was somehow involved with Fred's death? It was possible, and if true, their behavior supported her theory of a conspiracy either with Fred to kill himself or with a relative to kill Fred, money still the main motive for the crime.

What did she really know about Hark Bittersweet? Nothing beyond the surface facts of his style and demeanor. He was cool under pressure. He was not afraid to go against the flow, as shown by the way he intruded on her and Sam in the parlor.

The detective was either totally confident he would catch Fred's killer or totally confident he knew who the killer was and felt safe because they were in cahoots. Either way, Bailey was not completely comfortable with the man the local law enforcement obviously expected her and Sam to trust.

Now that Fred was gone, Bailey doubted she could ever hope to recapture the thrill she always experienced whenever she visited her uncle. No longer would her uncle excite her with tales of his travels around the world.

It was such a sad and ironic thing that he died in the arms of the one love that remained heartachingly beautiful until his bitter end, the Painted Lady. His death had brought something repulsive into the Painted Lady's air and now, everywhere that Bailey looked, she saw evil in the shadows.

Bailey realized she was shaking. She tried to relax, but her mind refused to be still. Questions churned in every corner of her psyche. What to do? Who to trust? Who did it? And why now? Why?

Somehow, she had to gain control of her negative thoughts, her wild impulse to run away from it all and keep on running. Somehow, she needed to feel more than strong, she needed to feel invincible. If she was scared and let it show, the killer would have a leg up on her, and Bailey had too much pride to let that happen.

So they decided to get away from the house for a little while, go out for coffee and conversation that could not be overheard by anyone else in the house. They were going to walk the streets as tourists and hold hands and forget, or at least pretend to forget, that Fred had been naked and alone in an electrified tomb of water and soap that no longer bubbled, and when they did leave the mansion, it felt wonderful.

On foot they traversed the downward slope of Dark Hill until they came to rest at the door of a tiny café where they drank strong black coffee in heavy white pottery, their hands cupping their mugs as if their fingers were cold. Fred was gone, his humor lost to them forever, and at the center of his death was the shock of a terrible mystery.

Sam watched tears fall down his wife's cheeks, and so he took a paper napkin from the table to wipe those tears away, all the love he felt for her evident in the tender way he pressed the rough, cheap paper against the soft flesh of her face.

A waitress refilled their cups with more steaming black brew and together, Sam and Bailey studied the fog that pressed hard against the windows of the little café whose name they had failed to catch.

TWELVE

Later, Bailey crossed the threshold into the blue room and closed the door. She looked around as if everything might have changed during their brief absence even if only a little bit; but the room remained unchanged, their borrowed bed and its covers and their personal artifacts still in the places she and Sam had left them.

It was the same guest suite, but it was the house that had changed. The house no longer welcomed or enchanted, no longer felt like the perfect place to begin a long, much overdue vacation, and in the borrowed bedroom she shared with Sam, a bowl of fresh fruit sat on an heirloom chest of polished ebony-colored wood. It looked so tasty that Bailey snapped off fat red grapes at random. A hybrid brand, the grapes were perfectly shaped and perfectly bland, a feast for the eyes but not for the tongue; she felt the same way about the house on Dark Hill.

The Painted Lady was a feast of the visual senses, rich colors and fine old furnishings, of tradition and heritage, but it was not a feast of joy for Bailey's emotions. Fred's strange and sudden death had altered her view of the Painted Lady, a place that had otherwise been a haven and source of rest for her.

Never again would she come to this home, a house of bitterness now, a house of regret. What game, she wondered, had Fred been playing, a game in which he had lost the greatest prize of all, his life? Bailey felt even more determined to solve the mystery of his death with whatever bits of truth she could find about the last days and moments of her uncle's life.

She had to do whatever it took to reach the truth, to gather it up in the form of hard facts, and to dispense the facts to the proper authority— in this case, the proper authority was Hark Bittersweet.

Yes, she would do whatever was necessary, she would take full advantage of every single opportunity that came her way, every chance that was useful, and cooking was useful. It served the purpose of feeding her soul and feeding her family, because even the emotionally twisted must eat or die.

Had she been at home, Bailey could have soothed her troubled soul through cooking until she had fully smoothed and eased her ruffled feelings back into place, but no matter how much she cooked in Fred's kitchen, there was no kitchen like the one in her own home.

The act of preparing good food for her family, of selecting ingredients, of slicing and dicing meat and vegetables, of ultimately putting the finished product on the table for consumption, was satisfying to her on a deeply spiritual level.

It rankled her nerves to think that the only people who would benefit from her cooking, besides herself and Sam, were her trifling relatives, none of whom had ever expressed an interest in her catering career, herself, or her family until now.

What her relatives did not understand was that Bailey needed to cook; for her, not cooking was like living life without the taste of chocolate, or the scent of ripe strawberries, the tang of lemons from her garden.

Before she left the Painted Lady a final time, Bailey planned to cook a final meal for her relatives, in memory of Fred who adored her culinary creations. So what if his burial arrangements, bought and stipulated many months before his death, stated that he wanted nothing special done in his memory? Cooking for Fred felt like the right thing to do.

Thinking about cooking made Bailey think about her daughters. Knowing they were safe at home with her in-laws gave her a sense of peace, of being grounded. Like a talisman, she thought of them often.

Should anything fatal happen to herself and Sam, it would be to those kind and generous people that the final rearing of the girls would fall upon, a task both Sam's parents would view as a labor of love, not simply an act of mercy. The senior Walkers' philosophy of giving and loving was the foundation of Sam's personality.

In every way in life that was important, Bailey mused, Sam had been there for her. When she had started her catering career making treats for birthday parties and dinner functions, he had been totally supportive.

When she worried about having limited funds for advertising, he told her that word of mouth was the best advertising of all, and he had been right. It was not long before she was able to add financial weight to the family income through catering, all without having to sacrifice time with her children, first Fern and later, Sage.

No longer was the catering business a hobby, it was a way of life, something Bailey would do whether she was paid for it or not. Sam understood this about her, the reason he had never offered her money to help her build her business, offering instead his praise and his helping hands, an encouragement she valued, respected.

In her sadness, Bailey analyzed her reflection in the mirror above the dresser. She had changed, profoundly, it was there in the wet sheen of her eyes, the subdued way she held her body in check.

She lifted her gaze, and there, beyond the reflection of herself in the huge oval mirror, its surface rimmed in polished granite, was the image of Sam. His face immobile, he too looked carved from stone.

It was as if he willed her to dig into the deepest parts of herself for courage, and she did dig, deep, right where it hurt the most—to do anything less was to be a coward. To be a coward now would shame them both.

In turn, it was Bailey's eyes that continued to arrest and enchant Sam. They were a deep ocher in color, warm and kind. Her brows were sleek and smooth against skin that was blemish-free, still supple and youthful in appearance.

Sam wished they had been in Italy when Fred's invitation had arrived. He had always wanted to take Bailey to Italy but had never made the time to get away from the office, something he sincerely regretted.

Had he and Bailey been in Italy, she would not be involved with the ugly side of her uncle's death, she would be able, then, to keep herself at a slight emotional distance, impossible now to do since she was the person who found Fred's body in the claw-footed bathtub she had once admired.

Bailey watched Sam through eyes that were wide and clear with a trust made solid over time and intimate experience, of home building and child rearing. His body smelled fresh from his recent shower, the scent of cocoa butter a slight whiff in the air. Of all the oils and creams she used to soften her body, it was cocoa butter Sam most often borrowed from her skin care collection.

His eyes were jet-black in color, his brows bushy and a little out of control. His mustache was groomed, the perfect complement to the strong, sensual lips she enjoyed nibbling many evenings in the privacy of their bedroom.

There were deep grooves carved into his cheeks by nature, the marks accentuated by age and time. In anger, Sam looked formidable. In love, he looked compelling. He was human, yes, but his basic goodness and kindness were what kept her love for him new.

Long before now, Bailey's passion for her only lover had mellowed into a subtle state of satisfaction, a satisfaction based on intense personal knowledge and profound compatibility. His body was thick and strong, reassuring in its strength. She felt no shame in her obvious need for him, no shame at all. She constantly exposed her secret self in gazes meant only for Sam, always for Sam.

He eased behind her, his heavy body a source of pleasure and solace in the richly dressed room that smelled of Bailey's perfume. He pulled her against him, her back to his front, and enjoyed the feel of her silk half-slip and matching black camisole, her body easily aligning itself to his form.

Sam hated the way she felt tense in his arms, tense and unhappy, more melancholy now than she had been at the start of their lovers' holiday. He said, "I'm gonna figure out who is behind this madness and nail him to the wall."

Bailey rolled her head, aware of a tight pain in her neck. Ever attentive, Sam used his powerful fingers to massage her tension away. From their many years of marriage together he knew exactly where to touch her, exactly where to be hard with his grip, where to be soft. In minutes, he felt the muscles beneath his kneading hands grow soft, her breathing more on an even keel as she leaned her weight harder against him.

"God," he said, "I love you."

Bailey rested against his chest, his arms around her now, his arousal pressed firmly against her body, as Sam used the force of his love to ease her troubled mind, his spirit to salve her aching heart.

Despite the disorder around them, their love for each other was a fine and genuine thing, and by coming to his wife this way, naked, honest, and giving, Sam bared more to her than his body and his love; he bared to her his soul, the sacred center of his being, the inner place where the true, the good, and the beautiful existed, sacred because in Sam's soul, evil had no chance to prevail.

Because evil never prevailed, Sam was able to safeguard his integrity, that special quality of absolute honesty that was the stuff of legend, stories in which ordinary men, like him, became heroes.

As his wife leaned against him, Sam treasured the gift of her trust, and was humbled by the knowledge that he and no other man was the hero in her life, the one man who made her feel convinced that the love story they lived was a tale of their own making.

For Bailey, Sam's unique brand of bravery radiated from his center, through the mass of his flesh, out of his body, and under her skin. Her faith in God was strong but it was Sam's physical self, his hard male body that she needed to cling to right now.

Breathing a sigh of satisfaction so deep that satisfaction was too minor a word for it, Bailey turned in her husband's arms. She pressed her breasts against his chest, felt the heat of his body through the expensive silk of her underwear.

As always, the desire to couple was there but the desire was tempered with a feeling that ran deeper than sheer lust, much deeper. What Bailey shared with Sam, in the sanctuary of their borrowed suite, was more than a rekindling of their marital union; instead, it was another chapter in the story of their life together.

Just as Sam lowered Bailey to the center of the four-poster bed, his intent to make love to her, the private telephone line rang in their suite. Reluctantly, he released his wife to answer the phone. Receiver in one hand, he sat on the side of the bed. "Hello?"

"It's me, Ridge." A homicide detective, Ridge Williams first met the Walkers when Bailey was attacked in the couple's home during the first murder mystery they solved together. Since that time, the Walkers had become good friends with the detective. They respected his opinion.

"Glad you got my message," Sam said.

"Vancy and I went on a much-needed vacation. Didn't get your message off the machine until now."

"No problem, man," Sam said to his old friend. "When I called your cell phone and didn't get through I figured you must have had something personal going on and would get back to me as soon as you could."

"Yeah," Ridge said. "Before I got married, I rarely took time off and when I did, I was always on call or easy to find. Thanks to Vancy, I'm not a workaholic anymore."

"She's been good for you."

"Yeah," Ridge said. "I know this isn't a social call. You said there's a problem. Sounded urgent."

Sam broke things down for him, concisely and without interruption. He told his friend about everything, beginning with the invitation, ending with the spreading of ashes. "Bailey is in danger. I feel it, Ridge."

"You don't trust anyone."

"Not even the police."

"I can be there within three hours."

"Hold off on that. I want you to look into the investigating officer here, a Hark Bittersweet. I don't have a good feeling about him."

"It's not like you to run off instinct alone, Sam. That's Bailey's area usually," Ridge said.

"True, but there's some logic behind it too. We've dealt with very few other area police officers since the murder, and to tell you the truth, I don't trust this guy is doing everything he can to find Fred's killer."

"You're convinced it's murder?"

"I am."

"Are Bailey's relatives really that bad?"

"Worse."

"I'll look into Bittersweet."

"Check with me later," Sam said, "say five o'clock."

"Yeah."

In slow motion, Sam replaced the receiver on its hook. He turned to face his wife. She was pissed.

Bailey said, "You didn't tell me you called Ridge."

"We need somebody on our side. Ridge is neutral in this case. He doesn't know anyone in your family and doesn't care whether he steps on any toes or not."

Bailey watched Sam dress in all black. "You still haven't explained why you didn't tell me you called him."

"You've got enough on your mind."

"We work together or not at all. You know that, Sam Walker. You can't shut me out, so don't even try."

"How can I shut you out when all I can think about is you?"

"Don't patronize me."

Sam placed his palms on her shoulder bones. "I won't fight you."

Bailey almost jerked away but stayed in his arms instead. "I'm sorry."

Sam pulled her against him, her breasts rising and falling fast against his chest. "Still, you're right. I should have told you I called Ridge."

"I'm glad you did call him though. . . ." Her pause was significant.

"But what?"

She laughed softly with irony. "You know me so well."

He kissed her on the top of the head. "But?"

"By calling in Ridge for help, even though right now his help is behind the scenes, I feel as if there's no hope for my family."

"Not every family is close, Bailey. You know that."

"True. I guess that's why I work so hard at keeping our little unit strong. I think of your parents as if they were my own. Having faith in your parents keeps me from worrying about the girls, too."

Sam squeezed her tight. "Nothing is gonna happen to us."

"I feel like we're in a bad movie."

"Me too."

Bailey squeezed him one last time, then broke their embrace. She wanted to stay on track. "You were very specific when you talked to Ridge. I hadn't realized you were that suspicious of Hark Bittersweet."

"He's a close friend of the family and right now everybody in the family is a suspect, so yeah, I'm suspicious. I like him even less than the other relatives. They've been ridiculous all along. This detective, and I use the word loosely, is supposed to be objective about everything he hears and sees. How can he be when he's this close to the victim? He hangs out in the parlor almost as much as we do."

"I'm glad Ridge is checking him out."

"In the meantime, let's do some digging. I don't like being passive in this investigation. Waiting for this Bittersweet character to do the right thing might wind up exploding in our faces. We can't afford to trust anyone but Ridge at this point."

"I agree," Bailey said.

Sam felt relief. "I'm glad you agree with me. I don't like being at odds with you. Come on. Let's call the girls."

"Since we don't trust anyone at Dark Hill, let's use our cell phone."

"Great idea."

It took several minutes to speak with each girl, then ten more to update Sam's parents with the details that could not be passed on to the girls. As far as the children were concerned, all was well with their parents.

After their phone call was finished, Bailey took a cleansing breath, held it several seconds, then expelled it with a whoosh. "I hate it that they heard about Fred's death on the news before we could tell them about it."

"My parents handled things well."

"You're right," Bailey said. "Since we've been involved with two other murder investigations, the girls are fully aware that bad things happen to good people, in this case, Uncle Fred."

"Mom had a bad dream about you last night," Sam said. "She's terrified. Dad told me she thinks the dense fog is unnatural."

Bailey stared out the window. The fog was coming back. Condensation pressed against the windows, to block out the world. A repressed sense of excitement dominated the mood within the richly decorated walls of the Painted Lady, and Bailey moved forward with both eyes open, both ears on the alert for the unusual and the damning.

She was at the end of her temper; the rope tethering her good manners in place was a single strand away from fraying altogether. She could not understand how they all had come to be in the predicament they shared and she felt anxious, her feelings scraped together by sheer force of will and the sturdy support of Sam.

THIRTEEN

Tuesday morning

Almost blind in their search for truth and justice, Sam and Bailey tackled the least likely suspects first, beginning with the maid. Fiesta Clark sat with the Walkers in the kitchen.

"Thank you for coming in today," Sam said.

"I just can't believe what's happening," Fiesta said. "The main reason I agreed to come here is that I don't believe Fred killed himself. I cleaned his bathroom, for God's sake. He didn't use a blow-dryer for any of his body parts."

Sam leaned forward. "So where did it come from?"

"A guest suite. Yours in fact."

"I assume you shared this information with Detective Bittersweet," Sam said.

"I did."

"And?"

"Well," Fiesta said, "the secondary reason I agreed to come here is that I don't trust Hark."

If Sam was surprised, he hid it very well. He weighed the woman and her words with care, then said, "So? You're on a first-name basis with him?"

"We weren't too formal around here."

"You don't consider either me or Bailey suspects in Fred's death, do you?"

"If I believed that," Fiesta said, "I wouldn't be talking to you."

"Why do you think we're innocent?"

"I've seen the two of you together," Fiesta said. "Real love, that's what I see. It's what Fred saw too."

For the first time, Bailey was compelled to speak. "You were in love with him weren't you?"

"I was."

"Was the age difference the stumbling block for the two of you?"

"I'm forty years his junior," Fiesta said. "Yeah. It was a problem. I'm also the maid. Can you imagine how Fred felt, being the owner of such finery and having a thing for the maid? He said it was too tired a notion, and he was too old to get into it all. I actually have a loft apartment downtown, totally paid for. I drive a Lincoln Continental. Paid for. All courtesy of Fred Durham. We were as close as we could be emotionally."

Sam kept his tone gentle. "Why did you keep working for him when you knew Fred didn't want to go public with your relationship?"

Fiesta stared off into the distance. "It was the only way I could be near him. The only way he would allow me to be near him. We talked a lot. I know about his deepest thoughts and feelings. Fred said there aren't a lot of people with hearts of gold, but you two have that quality about you. He loved you. If his murder can be solved, I believe it has to be done from the inside out. It's a family thing. Fred would want to keep this mess in the family."

"That's why you and the rest of the family are putting up with Hark Bittersweet," Sam said.

"Yes."

"In a way," Bailey said, her tone thoughtful, "that doesn't make sense. Fred was too well known in the Bay Area for the circumstances of his death not to be an issue. Everybody wants to know exactly what happened to him. Nothing can be kept a secret. There are reporters everywhere."

"But," Fiesta said, "details can be hushed and given out on a need-to-know basis. That's where Hark Bittersweet fits in best."

"I can see that," Sam said.

Bailey went to the maid. She cupped both of the woman's hands within her own. "Thank you for coming in today. I understand Fred's death is a shock and hardship for you."

"You know," Fiesta said, "it's not so much a shock."

Bailey's face showed her surprise. "Because of his age?"

"Yes. Fred had cancer. He refused to treat it."

"Why?" Sam asked.

"He said when it's time to go, it's time to go. He didn't want chemotherapy."

Bailey was stunned. "I had no idea."

"You weren't supposed to know."

"Did he tell anybody else?" Sam asked.

"I doubt it. I know because of our intimate relationship. I was his maid, so I saw the inside of his life. I was his companion, so I saw the inside of his heart. We talked freely together."

"Why wouldn't Malinder Simmons tell us about the cancer, or even Detective Bittersweet?" Bailey asked.

"Fred instructed Mal not to say anything. Don't

forget, he arranged his cremation well in advance of his death. Hark has his own motives for keeping silent about Fred's health. Like I said, Hark operates on a need-to-know basis."

"Point taken," Sam said.

"Also," Fiesta said, "you might want to talk to his secretary, Joan Harrington."

"We'll do that," Sam said.

Thirty minutes later, the maid was gone and the secretary was sitting in the same chair. "I knew about their closet affair," she said.

Bailey poured the secretary a cup of Constant Comment tea, which she served with a slice of orange. Joan had an air of honesty about her that Bailey found appealing. She sensed the other woman truly wanted to help. "Did anyone else know?"

"Maybe, but to tell you the truth," Joan said, "I only know because I worked closely with them. Everybody else just came around for money. They circled Fred like vultures waiting for their victim to die."

Sam said, "So you think someone killed him?"

"It wouldn't surprise me."

Bailey said, "Who do you think did it?"

Joan used an antique silver spoon to stir her tea, its aroma a cozy scent at the table. She spoke quietly, a delicate, almost imperceptible layer of sarcasm in her voice. "Isn't that what you're here to find out?"

Ever attentive to anything that might backfire in his or Bailey's face, Sam pounced on the sarcasm. "You don't like us asking questions."

"I don't like all the drama," Joan said. "Fred was good to me. Very generous. I'm a struggling writer, and he let me live in the gardener's cottage out back for free in exchange for my clerical services. It was like he was my patron. Like in the bad old days when authors and artists had people support them while they studied their craft."

"And the rest of the family knew about this special arrangement. I mean, that you worked without pay?" Bailey said.

"No."

"Why was it a secret?" Bailey asked.

"Fred was like that," the secretary said. "He did a lot of things in secret."

"Not according to the maid," Bailey said.

"Well, their relationship was a bit different."

"Let me get this straight," Sam said. "Fred supported his maid in exchange for her companionship. He supported you in exchange for clerical services." He paused to choose his words carefully. "Just out of the goodness of his heart."

"Yes," the secretary said. "That's exactly what I'm saying. You see, Fred was concerned about the quality of writing being produced today. He said that good writing, as an art form, is being replaced by flat-out commercialism. That kids don't read, not because of the Internet or video games, but because the material offered to them is lousy. Not everybody wants to read Alice Walker three times in a row in order to figure out her meaning. I like her work, but sometimes people want to read for escape, and I'm one of those people. Not just commercial quick fiction like, say, James Patterson, but something a little deeper, something that isn't full of choppy sentences or broken thoughts or a series of one-liners posing as paragraphs."

Bailey smiled. "You feel pretty strongly about this."

"So did Fred," Joan said. "It's the reason we

bonded so well. I couldn't afford to write the way I wanted to write: slowly, carefully, and still keep a solid roof over my head. Fred always said we were either throwbacks to a more artsy era, or renegades in a keenly capitalist one."

Bailey laughed. "I can hear him saying the word *keenly.*"

The secretary's laughter quickly turned to anger. "Fred didn't deserve to die the way he did."

"Did you know he had cancer?" Sam asked.

"No. As sorry as I am to hear he kept such a sickness secret, cancer didn't kill Fred. Find out which one of those selfish bastards did it."

Sam studied the secretary for a moment. "How do you feel about Detective Bittersweet?"

Joan wore a thoughtful expression. "Hark? He's good as gold."

"Somehow," Bailey said, "I don't believe you mean that."

"Believe it. Hark Bittersweet is so conscientious it turns my stomach to watch him in action."

"He's very intense," Bailey said.

"Humph," Joan said. "Intense about Fred's money. I'd say he's as disappointed as everyone else in the family that Fred left his estate to the both of you."

Sam said, "Why would he be upset when he isn't a Durham?"

"Fred donated money to charities that were handpicked by Hark. Hark had a certain level of prestige on Dark Hill because he was closely connected to Fred on a business level. Through Fred, Hark was able to hobnob with the rich and famous."

"I see," Bailey said. "Now that Fred is gone,

Hark won't have access to the funding he's used to getting for his pet projects."

"A step down in the private sector," Sam said.

"That's what I think," Joan said. "He had a lot to lose by Fred's death. I think Hark's in a hurry to find Fred's killer because he wants somebody to pay for screwing up his fund-raising meal ticket."

"I wouldn't put it quite that way," Bailey said, "but I figure pretty much the same thing. Except . . ." She paused to think her next words through. "Except the rest of the family had something to lose also. As long as he was alive, everyone's meal ticket was still in good standing."

"If we think like that," Sam said, "then greed wasn't the motive for Fred's murder, anger was."

"I'll buy that," Joan said. "The way I understand it, Fred put Sam in charge of his corporation and you, Bailey, in charge of this house and the various charities relating to children. He wants the community center to stay open, for example, but he left no provision in his will for the botanical gardens."

"The what?" Sam said.

"The public flower garden on Dark Hill," Joan said. "Fred wasn't into flowers much, and he agreed to it for a community development project back when Dark Hill was first being noticed by yuppies. I guess he figured that the community has built up to the point where current residents can handle the gardens if they want to keep them up. The kids and the community center are something different."

"The bottom line," Sam said, "is that Fred cut Hark out of his will just like he cut out the rest of the relatives."

Hark Bittersweet entered the kitchen. He tossed

his suit jacket over the back of a chair. "You're correct. I believe Fred died because he was taunting certain members of his family with disinheritance, knowing all the while that he'd already done that very thing. At one time, everyone in the family was set to inherit roughly equal shares."

"So," Sam said, "what prompted him to cut everybody out?"

"I wish I knew," Hark said. "Knowing I'm a homicide detective by trade, the relatives aren't opening up to me as usual. As you know, just about everyone is a suspect."

"Just about?"

"I've ruled out Joan, the maid, and the landscape people, and you two. Based on what I've witnessed and heard, none of you have the killing instinct."

"The what?" Bailey said.

"The mental turn-off switch it takes to kill, say for sport. You, Bailey, are more likely to go home and cook in order to burn off stress. You aren't likely to kill someone as a form of anger management."

"Give me a break," Bailey said.

"I'm serious," Hark said. "After murder, a killer with his moral switch off is more likely to get a bit more bold, a bit less careful."

Sam said, "You're looking for evidence in the form of words or attitude among a group of potential killers."

"Sam!" Bailey said.

"He's right," Hark said. "That's exactly what I'm doing. What I've got here is a group of people who all want the same thing: money. The money was denied them by one person: Fred. His denial activated somebody's rage. The rage pushed somebody to commit murder. It's up to me to sift through the switches."

"Trouble is," Sam said, "you had just as much reason to kill Fred as anybody else. I know Bailey and I are innocent. I doubt the maid or the secretary did it."

The only detective Bailey knew who could solve a crime without ever leaving home was Miss Marple. She wondered if Miss Marple ever felt the same level of frustration she felt right now. She said, "We're going around in circles, solving nothing. He killed himself. He didn't kill himself."

The detective squared eyes with Sam. "No, not exactly circles. We understand each other now. Your husband thinks I'm Fred's killer."

"It's part of your profession to kill if necessary," Sam said.

"Whatever you believe, believe this: I'm good at my job. I'm as interested in the truth as you are. I owe that, as a minimum, to Fred. I'm willing to sacrifice your privacy and your time to find out why Fred died."

Joan clapped her hands, slowly. "I need a napkin to wipe my tears."

Horrified, Bailey gasped.

The detective bowed his head slightly in Joan's direction. "I like knowing what I'm dealing with." To Sam, he said, "When I started this case, I thought it was open and shut. It's not. I retire in two days, and to be completely honest, I want this mess dealt and done with."

"I hate thinking that this wonderfully restored old mansion harbored so much hate," Bailey said. "Durhams have always been a bit eccentric, but none of us have been killers."

"None of us are born killers," the detective said.

"Most of us start off the same way: healthy. That's why I'm wading through dead ends here and why you feel you're going in circles. The family itself is the only suspect, collectively speaking, that is. That's also why all the leads are dead ends."

"I don't trust you," Sam said.

"I trust you, even though you've got your switch turned off."

Bailey was shocked. "How dare you!"

"Oh," the detective said, "I dare a lot of things. Only one man in this room is ready to wring somebody's neck, and it's not me. I've been around enough crime and violence to understand that you wouldn't be with him, Bailey, if Sam was as mean as he looks right now."

Sam rolled his eyes over the ever-present detective the same way he would a strange snake in the grass. "I'm not into keeping secrets."

The detective's smile was so slight there was hardly a glimpse of his professionally whitened teeth. "The fact that you've been interviewing suspects in the kitchen shows how much he respects you, Bailey. He should be out in the suspects' environments, the maid's home, the secretary's living quarters, their turf, not yours."

"This isn't my kitchen."

"But it is your domain. Your comfort zone. He's in this room right now because he loves you. You love the truth. The truth is why I'm here."

"I'm having you investigated," Sam said.

"Fine," the detective said, "but has it ever occurred to you that I'm trying to save Bailey's hide? With Fred dead, who do you think is next in line for murder?"

The news was unexpected, unwanted, and there was little time to think about its consequences.

Thank God for Sam, for his bulldog way of staying in everybody's face, whether he sat in the corner of a room, roamed by her side, or stood alone near a window, always with Bailey in full view, everyone around her under his acute, unrelenting suspicion.

It was as if he dared anyone to try to harm her, dared anyone to try anything out of the norm, just once, just so he would be able to excuse himself for venting his anger at the desperate situation he and Bailey found themselves fighting with all their wits gathered tight around them. Sam's very presence challenged every Durham to stay on guard, from him, and from each other.

FOURTEEN

It was early Wednesday afternoon. Sam and Bailey had just returned from the reading of Fred's will at Malinder Simmons's office, located in downtown San Francisco. They were in their suite.

"It's time for a dinner party," Sam said.

Bailey eyed him as if he were crazy. "A what?"

Sam's mouth was set, his features hard, but as cruel as he looked, Bailey did not fear him. It was Sam that she wanted, Sam that she had, in the form of his integrity, his security, and ultimately in his physical self.

With him, her desperate feelings of anger were less overwhelming, her grief more vulnerable than incapacitating. He kept her thoughtfully in the present, in the heat of the drama and the passion that was the foundation of Fred Durham's life.

"You heard me right. A dinner party. A get-together. Whatever you want to call it. We need to get everybody in one place. Food and drink seem to be the easiest method to accomplish this goal. We haven't had everybody at the table at the same time since the first night we got here. That includes Hark Bittersweet."

"It's sounds so callous," Bailey said, "to invite people to dinner after the reading of the will. We didn't have a dinner after the funeral, for Pete's sake."

"We're stranded, first by the dense fog, now by a sense of duty. I say we do whatever it takes. We've served dinner, breakfast, and snacks so far, but it's been haphazardly done. The first dinner was planned by Fred, and we were surprised by who attended. Breakfast has been informal with people helping themselves or not eating at all. We've cooked dinner but didn't formally invite everyone to attend. I think we should do that. Get formal. We're down to the wire with Hark Bittersweet's retirement happening this Friday.

Bailey said, "Friday is our wedding anniversary."

"Friday we'll be driving down the coast looking forward to the future. This case will be solved. Once this case is solved, the healing can begin."

"You sound so positive."

"I am."

"You've been thinking about this final gathering for some time, haven't you? Sort of like a grand finale."

Sam was quick to respond. "Ever since we found out from Joan Harrington that Fred named you the soul beneficiary of his estate. Right then, I figured other people knew positively that Fred had cut everybody else out of the will. It wasn't really a closely kept secret. It made sense that you would be the killer's next target. Bittersweet is right about that."

Bailey massaged her temples. "This is a nightmare. I wanted adventure, but not like this."

"All the answers we want are in this house. We just have to keep our minds and our eyes open until we're satisfied."

"The odd thing, Sam, is that I'm not afraid anymore even though I probably should be. I was, but now I'm just ticked off."

Sam eased her into his arms. "Now I'm the one who's scared. If something happens to you, I'll be directly responsible because it's my job to protect you."

Bailey squeezed him tight. "You've hardly left my side. You're suspicious of everyone, including the police. You've alerted an outside law official, Ridge, to what's going on up here. If someone tries anything now, that person will surely be caught quickly. I'm as safe now as I would be at any other time."

"I disagree," Sam said. "Anyone cunning enough to kill Fred in his own bathtub with a blow-dryer he didn't need—which, by the way, I think is a joke on the killer's part—is cunning enough to go after you. Multimillions are at stake here. I'd say whoever is behind all the drama going on would get a kick out of destroying you while I'm standing by. Without you, I'd be like Samson with his hair cut off, blind and scarred for life."

"Let's hurry and get this mess over with. I can't even grieve properly with all this stuff going on," Bailey said.

"Agreed."

"But, Sam, don't you think it's strange nobody is trying to go home? Like us, they come and go throughout the day but everybody always returns."

"I think people are staying because of the suspense. Like us, nobody wants to be left out of the mix."

Bailey could not completely let go of her conspiracy theory. "What if they're all in it together, Sam? What if I was set up from the beginning to take the fall, only our reputation as amateur detectives gave us some credibility in Detective Bittersweet's eyes?"

"I'd agree with you if it hadn't been for Fred's invitation. I think Fred knew someone was out to get him. The invitation is your alibi to be here as a witness."

Bailey paced a few tense steps, then returned to Sam. "Witness to what?"

"His state of mind. His behavior."

"A ruthless move."

"A ruthless man," Sam said. "Fred amassed his fortune carefully, with an intensity that made no room for a wife or children or even a steady girlfriend. If you take away the fact that you loved Fred the man, you would be left with the basic truth of his personality: He was self-centered. Selfish with his time, he gave money instead. It's little wonder to me that your relatives are pissed off about being cut out of the will. It was their prime connection to Fred, the money man. With no children to pass on his fortune, they all figured the money would be left to them. It wasn't. Maybe somebody was banking on a high influx of cash at some point."

Bailey came clean with a truth of her own. "To be honest, I had hoped Fred would leave me the house. I would have liked to keep it in the family, but now, you couldn't pay me to hang on to this place. It's a killing place."

"What about the furnishings?"

"I think we ought to make use of the things we'd like to hang on to for the girls, in honor of the Durham name, which after all is my heritage and theirs. The rest, we can divvy among the surviving relatives or auction off. I'm willing to share what's here."

"Even though Fred might not have wanted it this way?"

"He probably did. If he left everything to me, he had to have known I wouldn't have wanted it because of the excess. We're both successful and pretty much happy with our lives. We don't need all this stuff."

"We were stagnant."

Bailey laughed softly. "I wouldn't mind some of that comfort right now."

"Let's get dinner going."

"Let's."

Hours later, Bailey was in the dining room. She set the table with Durham family silver, a heavy American brand, emblazoned with the letter D, in flowing script. There was ivory china from Germany, rimmed in twenty-four-karat gold. The Spanish glassware was a cut-lead crystal, rimmed in gold to match the plates.

As always, Bailey operated with a to-do list. She laid out the main and side dishes. On the sideboard, she placed the dessert along with appropriate china and flatware. She set the candles aflame in silver Portuguese candleholders, and turned the locally crafted crystal chandelier down to low. After making sure the linen-draped table looked balanced, Bailey stepped back to admire her handiwork.

"Everything looks wonderful, sweetheart," Sam said. While she had been cooking, he had notified the relatives that dinner would be served at seven.

"I feel good. Glad you suggested this for tonight."

Sam held his wife in his arms. She smelled like

the perfume she favored but the familiar fragrance was joined by the scents of the excellent food she had prepared with expert hands. He smelled everything she had created, the meats, the vegetables, the hot butter on the bread, the pastry, the drinks.

Sam inhaled a deep breath, then blew it out on a hard sigh. "If it wasn't for Fred's murder, this would be a perfect evening."

"I know."

"The great thing about tonight—and this setting—is that it's relaxing. Relaxed people have loose tongues. Maybe we'll hear or see something useful, something that will help us solve this case."

"I just can't believe that we're referring to Uncle Fred as a case. I hate this."

"You turned your hate into the makings of this terrific meal. Regardless of the nasty way your off-the-wall relatives are behaving, I bet all but one of them will feel the same way, uplifted."

"The exception is Fred's killer."

"Yeah."

"You, know," Bailey said, "I've been trying to remember if Fred was ever in a violent situation before. He was. He and Dexter's father got into it once. Fred threw Dexter's dad against a wall and told him to get out."

"What were the men fighting about?"

"I was a kid and it was summer, like this," Bailey said. "I remember because it was the first time I had ever seen grown people physically fighting. The weather was odd, like this. Only then, there was rain. It rained so hard the grounds and surrounding streets flooded. The men were fighting over money."

Bailey spoke in a faraway tone, as if her mind's

eye had returned to that long-ago summer in her youth.

"Dexter's dad wanted money?"

"Not exactly. He told Uncle Fred that he hung his will—the Durham family inheritance—over everybody's heads like a carrot: Do what I want, get what you want. What everybody wanted was Uncle Fred's millions. He wanted people to want him for himself."

"Fred claimed to want people to want him for himself but what you're saying is that when Dexter's father didn't kiss up to your uncle, Fred didn't like it," Sam said.

"Yep. Basically, Dexter's dad turned away from the family fortune, but his wife didn't. She kept Dexter in Uncle Fred's face. She figured that Uncle Fred's fortune was her son's legacy, and she was determined he'd get it. At some point, Dexter's dad died. Dexter and his mother lived off the trust fund Uncle Fred set up for them. Along the way, Dexter became the perennial playboy. No one in the family takes him too seriously. I know I don't."

"I take him seriously," Sam said. "I don't trust him in my sight or out of it. A man in his thirties who doesn't earn a respectable living off his own mind and his own two hands isn't worth much in my eyes."

"I hear you," Bailey said. "Money makes a huge difference in people's lives. I suppose it's reasonable to think Dexter might have panicked when Uncle Fred tossed him out of the will. He has no formal trade or training. When you look as good as he does, it's not too hard to be a gigolo."

"Like the maid and the secretary, Fred left your relatives with nothing after his death. He gave generously in life, so he probably felt he'd done enough. Except for you. You've never asked anything of him."

"Didn't Jackie Onassis do something like that, I mean provide for her sister during life and left nothing after she died?"

"I had heard that. Don't know if it's true though," Sam said, his manner nonchalant. "Whether it is or isn't, I can understand the reasoning. It's like living in a house for free while you make millions. What do you do with your millions? Splurge every day on your wants? Or do you make long-term provision for your needs? Fred must have figured he had provided well for those people and if they didn't plan something positive and meaningful for their future then that was their problem."

"Yeah, kind of like that Grisham book, *The Testament*. The business tycoon in the story left all his money to the one relative who had never asked anything of him. In this case, that would be me."

"A poetic justice and irony," Sam said.

"Yes. I suppose that would appeal to Uncle Fred's sense of humor. If it wasn't happening to me, I'd think it was fair. I say fair because the money wouldn't be wasted. I wouldn't squander the funds he provided. He must also have known that you would safeguard the corporate end of his . . . empire, I don't know what else to call it."

"Empire is right. He probably died because of this decision."

"I feel guilty," Bailey said, her voice so hushed Sam had to strain to hear her. "How can I enjoy Uncle Fred's gift without remembering how I got it?"

"It's not so much an enjoyment, Bailey, as it is

a duty. I won't push you. You can give every penny of the money away to charity if you want or you can do as Fred did, which was to support your relatives, but what I encourage you to do is think. To think, you need time and a clear mind. In order to get to that point, we've got to find the exact truth about Fred's death. After that, we'll talk in more detail to his lawyers and other advisors. Then you can make your decision."

"You sound like you want the money."

"I have everything I need, Bailey. If nothing else, Fred's death highlights how important you are to me. As sentimental as it sounds, for me, our love runs deeper than death. Stronger. Let's face it. We've been broke. We've been well off. We've been broke again. Through it all, we've had each other. That's all I've ever really needed or wanted. The girls will grow up and leave us someday to build their own families. It's you I'm gonna grow old with. It's you I'm gonna stand by right now. You," he said with emphasis, "are my fortune."

"Fortune," Bailey said. "I guess that since it was important to Fred, it ought to be important to me. Man, I hate being in this predicament."

"The way I see it, you need to decide if you want to expand on his legacy. If you do, I'm with you. If you don't, I'm with you. Fred wasn't my uncle. My only connection to his money is you. I've never had access to it, and I've never given it much thought."

"But you would keep it if the decision was yours to make."

"I would."

"Why?"

"Because of the hardship it took to make it. Because of the hardship to keep it. Then there's the death Fred suffered to manage it. It's like thousands of acres of land purchased say a hundred years ago in the South by a sharecropper, a son of a former slave. Say the land was passed down for generations until the last of the line had to decide what to do with it. Keep it or sell it. Selling it is kind of like selling the dream. On the other hand, the dream had been achieved and shared by generations, and therefore, the original goal— to own a vast amount of land and pass it on—had been achieved."

Bailey paced off, then returned to Sam. "I see both sides of the question: to sell or not to sell. I agree that now isn't the time to make that decision. Let's stick to finding the final details to Uncle Fred's death. Dinner tonight ought to be an eye-opening experience."

"Am I invited?" the detective asked upon entering the suddenly hushed room.

Sam's top lip twitched. "How long have you been standing there eavesdropping, Bittersweet?"

"Long enough. I repeat, am I invited?"

"Of course," Bailey said, her gaze roaming the ever neat, ever watchful detective. "Have you found out anything interesting about Uncle Fred?"

"My commanding officer thinks you did it, Bailey. Unless you come up with a signed confession or some other strong evidence to clear your name, my commanding officer is convinced this case is open and shut. It's your goody-two-shoes background that's saving your hide right now. That and the fact Fred spoke highly of you."

Sam glared at him. "Time is running out."

"There never was any time," the detective said,

his ordinary face looking extraordinarily tired.
"Haven't you figured that out yet?"

That night, dinner was uneventful. Everyone was
polite, so polite that Bailey worried this meal was
the calm before the storm.

FIFTEEN

Wednesday night

In Sam and Bailey's guest suite, the phone rang. It was their good friend, Ridge Williams. "I didn't find anything criminal or otherwise negative about Hark Bittersweet," he said to Sam once the usual pleasantries had been spoken.

"While I'm glad to hear that," Sam said, "I have to wonder what it is I don't trust about that guy. Every time we turn around the bastard is standing there."

"I understand he's a loner," said Ridge. "Divorced. Childless. Solid professional record. Close to retirement and ready for it. I suppose it's possible Bittersweet killed Fred in order to go out with a bang. You know about the saying truth is stranger than fiction."

Sam thought for a minute, then said, "If Bittersweet planned the murder, he'd need a scapegoat."

"Bailey."

"It's easy enough to chuck a blow-dryer in the bathtub and wait for somebody to holler for help, which is exactly what happened."

"My sources say Bittersweet's superiors think Bailey did it."

"If they do, it's probably because he suggested it," Sam said. "If he suggested it, he'd have something to gain."

"Notoriety."

Sam nodded in agreement even though his friend could not see him. Theirs was a friendship that ran along the lines of brothers, without the tension of true sibling rivalry, which Bailey was experiencing now with her family. "That would be my guess since Hark isn't getting any money out of Fred's will."

"I don't like you two staying in that house," Ridge said.

"There's no guarantee we'll be out of danger if we leave. Nobody's leaving, which I think says a lot."

"What's your time limit for staying on Dark Hill?"

"Bittersweet's last day on the job this week," Sam said. "He's burning to solve this case, and so am I. The only trouble with staying with Bailey's crazy relatives is that I'm almost too close to the action to be objective."

"You have to be objective," Ridge said in a warning tone. "You could easily miss a clue if you aren't."

"That fact has me looking over my shoulder and behind every door. It'll be hard to take me by surprise, Ridge. I'm ready for anything."

Ridge paused several beats before saying, "Which means you're examining everything that makes Bailey look guilty."

"Exactly."

"It's a dangerous way to tackle the problem," Ridge said.

"I don't know any other way. I tried looking at the problem with Fred killing himself, with somebody killing Fred, with somebody planning to kill him only he beat them to it out of spite. The only thing I'm sure of is Fred didn't die by accident. If the appliance found in the tub had been a radio, I might have gone along with the accident angle, but a fingerprint-free blow-dryer in the tub of a bald man is too bizarre to be accidental. Fred was as wacky as the rest of his relatives but only in an eccentric way."

Ridge was silent a moment before saying, "What do you mean?"

"The Durhams are nosy, well-read people. I've heard the John Grisham book come up more than once. Fred probably read the same book Dexter and Bailey did. It's a best-seller. Anyway, Fred had cancer, and he was dying, which is similar to the rich guy in the book. Maybe the book was the source of Fred's idea to kill himself and turn the screws on his relatives while he was at it."

"Are you talking about *The Testament*?"

"Yeah."

"Vancy read it and told me about it. She keeps referring to doing things on Brazilian time, as in tomorrow. That's why I stopped carrying my cell phone everywhere and how I missed your original mayday call when Fred died."

Sam laughed. "Brazilian time, huh?"

"Yeah. My wife is never boring."

"Tell her hello for me."

"Just stay close to Bailey."

"I will."

"You know, you can work this case from New Hope," Ridge said. "There's no legal reason for you to stay in that house. You aren't under house arrest, and even though it's been pretty foggy out there, the fog hasn't stopped travel."

"We know this. Everybody does. I just think people are afraid that whatever happened to Fred could happen again to any one of them. Everything gets back to Bailey. She stands out whether she opens her mouth or not, whether she takes any action or not. All eyes are on her and believe me when I tell you those eyes are treacherous."

"I hear you," Ridge said. "She wasn't after Fred's millions but she got them. She didn't kill her uncle but she's the number-one suspect. She could leave the Painted Lady but if she did, Fred's killer could easily finish her frame-up."

"Exactly," Sam was quick to point out. "I don't think anyone realizes how truly nosy Bailey is as a rule."

"What are you getting at, Sam?"

"Even if Fred wasn't her uncle, she'd have been curious enough about his death to stick around for the facts. She's just nosy enough to be a danger to the real culprit regardless of where she lives simply because she won't let the matter drop. The medical examiner said suicide. Bailey's nose tells her otherwise, and I agree with her. That's why I think the real killer is still in this house. Whoever it is can't afford to let her out of sight."

"Huh," Ridge said, as if he was finally getting the full picture of what the Walkers were scrabbling to deal with on Dark Hill. "Kind of like an arsonist watching a building he set on fire burn to the ground."

"Yeah."

"Watch yourself, my friend."

"I will. With me out of the way, Bailey makes for an easier target."

"You wouldn't have to be killed to get to her," Ridge said, "just incapacitated in some way. It's a shame you're dealing with family. In a way it doesn't matter who the killer is. Fred's death hurt everyone."

"You know the saying about the love of money being the root of all evil."

"Yeah," Ridge said, a trace of bitterness in his voice, "but in this case, evil wears the face of someone you know."

"Tell me about it."

"One more thing, Sam, Fred had divested himself of his carriage business."

"Why didn't Bailey know about it?"

"She wouldn't unless someone told her. It's kind of like Colonel Sanders and Kentucky Fried Chicken. Basically, Fred was a logo, a front man, just like the colonel was a logo for KFC. Fred sold his carriage business years ago—are you ready for this?—to his competitor, Dexter's father."

"That doesn't make sense," Sam said.

Ridge laughed a little, his tone ironic. "It makes as much sense as everybody reading John Grisham. Life imitating art and all that."

"No one else in the family knows about this either, I gather."

"Not even Dexter," Ridge said.

"Why the secret?"

"I'm still digging." Ridge paused a few beats, as if he was reluctant to break contact with his stalwart, embattled friend. "Check you later."

"Right."

Sam hung up the heavy, ornate French phone and turned to Bailey. "You better sit down." She sat. When Sam finished repeating his conversation with Ridge, she was speechless.

"It's almost hard to believe," Sam said. "Fred must have been living off his investments and interest. This would explain why he didn't want to continue funding all the private organizations he was involved in. His resources were limited."

"Maybe. It makes sense."

"It's great to be on the same page."

Bailey forced a calm face. "Are we?"

Sam stilled at her tone. "What do you mean, are we?"

"You were talking to Ridge like I'm not in the room."

"Don't be ridiculous."

"Don't act like you don't know what I'm talking about."

"We can't afford to fight, Bailey."

"We can't afford to work this case on different sides. Our success in the past is because we worked together. Don't blow the mold."

He said nothing.

"Sam?"

A muscle worked in his jaw. "Talk."

"It was a shock to everybody's system to find out for sure that I'm the sole beneficiary of Uncle Fred's estate. To find out his manufacturing business is gone will really shake the family foundation."

Sam snorted in disgust. "What foundation? There is no foundation."

"You know," Bailey said, "this really does feel like a bad play."

Sam shook his head. "You'll have to explain that."

"Well, I'm thinking about Mary Stewart's novel, *Madam, Will You Talk?*, an old romantic suspense story set in France."

Sam gave her thigh a squeeze. "God, I love

the way your brain works. Agatha Christie. John Grisham. Mary Stewart."

She squeezed him back. "In the story, the heroine starts off her adventure by feeling as if she's a bit actor in a classic tragedy. You know the kind: sex, greed, murder, a killer lurking in the shadows."

"I follow."

Bailey grinned. "As I knew you would."

"Go on."

"Like Mary Stewart's heroine, I had no idea when we started our vacation we'd end up in the house from hell."

"Strong words for the Painted Lady," Sam said.

"In this case, her beauty is skin deep. Not a whole lot of people will want to live in this place once they find out a man was killed here. I know I don't want to live here, and Fred was my uncle."

Understanding dawned in Sam's mind. "You're planning to sell the mansion."

"Yes."

"Take time to think about it before making a final decision. Now isn't the best time." His attitude was solemn but encouraging.

"I enjoy the home we've built together," Bailey said. "Our girls were born there. We have friends in New Hope, but no, Sam, the Painted Lady isn't for me."

"You could give it to your lovely cousins."

"Who would sell it just the same. We'll use the money from the sale to put the girls through college and get them on their feet when they're done. If they don't go to college, we'll help them in some other way."

Sam's smile was crooked. "My mother would have a fit if she knew you weren't pushing the girls off to college when they finish high school."

"I know," Bailey said. "Your mother is a traditionalist down to the bone, and she raised a traditionalist son. She would argue that education is as vital to the American public as the right to vote. She might even say it's sacred."

"You disagree."

"I come from a family of entrepreneurs," Bailey said. "Uncle Fred inherited his wealth but he built on it with his own finesse. He wasn't college educated and neither am I. What I learned from him and other successful Durhams is that there's more than one way to skin a cat, so to speak."

"Do you realize we're rambling?"

Bailey laughed. "I'm tired."

"Let's get back to the case. The sooner it's solved, the sooner we can move on."

"Right," Bailey said. "Hark can't do it alone. If he could, he'd shut us down by saying we're screwing up an official police investigation."

Sam winked at her. "Damn, you're good."

"Thank you."

"Let's go after Sybil."

Bailey frowned. "Why?"

"She's the gossip in the family."

"The second most nosy, you mean, me being the first, of course."

"That too."

They walked out of their guest suite and straight into Hark Bittersweet.

"Sam. Bailey," the detective said, "I was just looking for you."

Sam was the first to speak. "Why?"

"Sybil is dead."

SIXTEEN

"If this is your idea of a sick joke," Bailey said, "you've got a lot of nerve." She wondered if fear made her reckless enough to speak the way she did.

"I don't joke about death, young lady," the detective said.

Bailey had a terrible time getting her mind to grasp the idea of another death, so soon after her uncle's murder. "We just had dinner. She hasn't been anywhere. How can she be dead?"

Sam squeezed her shoulder but directed his words to Hark Bittersweet. "What happened?"

"I don't know yet."

"But you have your suspicions," Sam said.

"I do."

"Go on."

"It appears as if Sybil was bashed over the head with a rolling pin."

Bailey shoved past the detective. She marched down the stairs, her steps hard and sharp against the floor. "That's ridiculous."

"The rolling pin is made of marble," the detective said, "solid marble." He spoke to her back.

Bailey stopped at the bottom landing but chose not to turn around. She was afraid to turn around lest the detective see the terror blazing bright in her pretty Durham brown eyes, a distinctive family trademark she had paid little attention to until now when she studied her family with such intense scrutiny. "Marble?"

The catch in her voice sent Sam speeding to her side. He desperately wanted to ease her anguish, but there was little he could do beyond offering her the full scope and tremendous power of his love. When it came to Sam's love for Bailey, the feeling was everlasting, one bound in honor and all the tender mercies known only between long-time lovers. He said, "Talk to me, baby."

"I used a marble rolling pin to make the dessert. I'd never used one before and chose it to make dessert tonight instead of the wooden pin that was also in the kitchen drawer. I like using wood and have one that your mother gave me when we married and so I've never been interested in the other types of rolling pins."

Sam pulled her into his arms, pressed his cheek against his chest, and said, "Hush, baby, everything's gonna be all right."

"I don't know about that," the detective said. "Bailey just admitted she handled the rolling pin today."

Sam glared at the detective. "She also has a solid alibi for having her fingerprints on that thing. She used it to cook dinner for a bunch of selfish bastards, and one of them is getting away with murder! Twice!"

The usually ultracalm detective grimaced. "There's no need to shout."

Sam's arms dropped away from Bailey's shoulders, his expression one of pure rage. He clearly wanted to wring the detective's neck. "Like hell there isn't!"

"Don't ever forget who you're dealing with, Walker," the detective said. He spoke quietly, authority heavy in his tone. His body remained loose and ready for anything. "Get control of yourself."

"He's right, Sam," Bailey said. "As much as we can't stand this guy, he is the man in charge of the . . . murders. I mean, of their investigation. He's right to think I'm a suspect both times. Someone's out to get me, Sam."

The detective scowled at Sam. "You don't have to like me, but you do have to work with me. My superiors—"

Sam cut him off. "To hell with your superiors. How do we know you're telling us the truth? How do we know you aren't the one setting us up!"

"Faith," Bailey said. "We have to believe God is on our side. To have faith, we have to have trust. To have trust, we have to believe that whatever is supposed to happen will happen, in its own time, in its own way."

"Destiny," Sam said.

"Whatever you want to call it," Bailey said. "It's true that we've never really been formal about our religious beliefs, but even so, we've always believed and have honored Him in our own way, in our own time. In a situation this impossible, we've got to trust He'll take care of us."

"All that may be well and good," the detective said, "but you're up against hard physical evidence like dead bodies and probable fingerprints on a marble rolling pin that will most likely be confirmed as the murder weapon in Sybil's death. I gave you my card, use it to contact me anytime.

My home address is on the back. I'm not the enemy here."

"Your point, Detective?" Bailey said. Her voice wavered a little. She felt an almost overwhelming urge to run.

"Use me," the detective said. "Trust me. I can help you."

Bailey's voice and face were ugly in the soft light of the stairway. "How can I do that when you're a suspect yourself?"

"I had nothing to gain by Fred's death," the detective said.

"We all had something to gain," Bailey said, a bit on the testy side. "We all had something to lose."

"But we aren't all the sole heir to a rich man's estate, someone who could be killing off the people who are most likely to contest Fred Durham's will. Don't," the detective said, "try to play hardball with me. Whether you like me or not isn't important. I am a homicide detective, and there is a murder investigation going on and your name keeps popping up."

Bailey spoke low and harsh. "This is insane."

"Even though I hate to admit it, Bailey," Sam said, "Detective Bittersweet is right. We do need to work with him."

All the fire left Bailey in a whoosh of emotion. She suddenly felt drained and humbled. "I'm going to jail," she said softly.

"Not while I'm still breathing," Sam said. He looked ready to spit fire. "Let's use the hell out of Bittersweet."

"To be honest, young lady," the detective said, "I'm the best chance you've got to get out of this mess."

"I have an alibi for using that rolling pin,"
Bailey said. "You can't forget that fact."

"True," the detective said. "But can you explain
why Sybil wrote your name on her bathroom mirror in blood?"

Bailey placed her face in her hands and cried.

Her husband said, "Enough standing around doing nothing but talking." He glared at the detective. "I assume you have a team of forensic people
on the way."

"I do."

Sam's mind was clicking at top speed, his brow
furrowed, his lips tight. "Where are the rest of the
relatives?"

"In the parlor. Drinking."

"I could use one of those," Bailey said. She
wiped her face with her hands, as if by doing so,
she could wipe away her troubles.

"You don't drink," the detective said.

"Thorough son of a—gun, aren't you?" Sam
said.

"Regardless of what you might want to believe,
I'm excellent at my job, and I'm excellent because
I take my work seriously," the detective said. He
handed Bailey a clean white cotton handkerchief
from his pocket. "I retire in a few days, and I want
this case closed. The secret to these murders is in
this house. It's why I keep hanging around. I also
think Bailey's life is at risk."

"If only the Painted Lady could talk," Bailey
said.

"Maybe she is," the detective said.

"In a sinister kind of way, I see what you mean,"
Sam said, his wife's deep melancholy mood having
struck a chord in him. "Everybody wants to go
home, but they don't want to go because of the

killing going on. Tempers are hot. Accusations are flying. I doubt anybody truly believes Bailey is the killer but with no evidence pointing to anyone else, she makes the perfect scapegoat. It's not like the killer wants to be caught."

"What if that's not the case?" Bailey said. She carefully folded the detective's handkerchief, then promptly wrung it between her hands. "What if the killer expects to be caught eventually, say by process of elimination? I've heard of AIDS victims who willingly infect as many people as possible before they die. Maybe this killer has that kind of mind-set. Maybe he wants to hurt as many relatives as possible before he's caught."

Sam took the handkerchief from Bailey, folded it, and stuck it in his own pocket. He wanted no other physical evidence from his wife in the detective's hands if he could help it. "And maybe the rest of us are sticking around in some macabre twisted way just to see what happens. We all know we aren't truly stranded, but like a horror movie filled with death and gore, we're staying until the grisly end of the drama."

Bailey beamed at him, her smile luminous and trusting. "Yeah."

"The last scene in the last act of the play," Sam said. He was thinking of Bailey's prior reference to Mary Stewart's novel, *Madam, Will You Talk?*

"All I know," Bailey said, "is that all this arguing isn't getting us anywhere. If I'm not careful, I'll be in jail over this mess. It's starting to look more and more like we're going to need a miracle to solve this case."

"Young lady," the detective said, "I am your miracle." The detective was fully aware that Sam had pocketed his handkerchief. He also knew why, but he let it slide. He had plenty of physical evidence from Bailey, especially in her guest suite and in the kitchen. He knew where she lived, he could get samples of her DNA from her home later if necessary. Most important, the detective believed in her innocence.

Bailey looked at him long. She looked at him hard. "I need a miracle all right," she said, "a big one."

Hours later, and after great discussion between themselves, the Walkers decided to take a chance on Detective Bittersweet and check him out on his own turf. The detective's home sat on a corner at the foot of Dark Hill and looked out over the botanical gardens that Fred's money had gone into over the years.

It was a large Victorian house that looked as if a fresh coat of paint was in order, yet the lawns were beautifully manicured, all green, all lush, and very inviting. The front entrance to the house was adorned with an American flag posted beside the front door.

The detective's house looked like a young couple's first-time home, a fixer-upper with loads of potential. It did not look like the type of home a retiring cop would call his own, a loner cop with no wife or children. It looked like prime real estate.

There was not much of a driveway, but there was room for Sam's sedan. Birds were singing in the trees and car horns were blaring in the background. Somewhere in the neighborhood, a small lawn mower was running, and the smell of grass was faint but present. The smell reminded Sam that it was summer, even in the habitually cool climate of San Francisco.

The detective answered the standard ding-dong of his doorbell. There was no way to tell, just by staring at Sam, that he was edgy. Sam hated to leave the Painted Lady, but he needed the fresh air, the distance, in order to maintain his objectivity, if one could call keeping his wife alive an objective goal.

It was his duty and privilege to do the right thing by her, which at the moment, was to consult with a man he was forced out of bitter necessity to trust.

The house Sam and Bailey entered was definitely male. It was a mixture of wine colors and dark woods, of framed black-and-white art featuring late jazz musicians. There was a huge black piano in the detective's parlor, only a piano, and Sam was inclined to ask the detective if the instrument was for show or for play, but this was not a social visit, therefore he declined to ask.

"Bailey," the detective said, "can I take your sweater?"

"No."

"Come," the detective said to the Walkers. "Join me on the terrace. It's cool but not too cold to enjoy. There's coffee."

Sam spoke for himself and his wife. "Thanks."

From the detective's terrace, the lawn mower could no longer be heard, and the sounds of constant traffic were restful, like the background noise of a television set turned on solely for its canned brand of company.

There was a conventional five-piece patio table ensemble, complete with umbrella, which was open. There was a silver thermos of coffee and three cups, no sugar or creamer, as if the detective sat waiting for the very guests he had just received.

On the narrow ledge of the short terrace wall, a heavy gray-blue cat slept in a sliver of sunlight, the sound of constant traffic the cat's lullaby.

Bailey smiled. "You knew we'd come."

"It's why I wrote my home address on the back of the business card I gave you after the funeral."

"I wanted to rip it up, but Sam wouldn't let me."

"Please," the detective said, "sit down."

Together, the Walkers and their ally sat beneath the open umbrella at the rectangular patio table and traded notes, together, they made plans to catch a killer.

SEVENTEEN

In the kitchen, Bailey felt like cooking up a storm, only she had no idea what she wanted to cook. She stood and stared blindly into space.

Tyra walked into the kitchen. "I can't believe you're standing there with a pot in your hand. Sybil's body is still warm, for Christ's sake. How can you think of cooking at a time like this? How?"

Almost absentminded, Bailey gazed at the aluminum Farberware cooking pot she had completely forgotten she was holding in her hands. What if the cooking pot turned up later at the scene of another Durham family crime? "The police won't let me near the body—"

Tyra was beside herself with gall. She could hardly contain all the animosity she felt. "And they shouldn't, you friggin' know-it-all."

"I want to see what happened for myself," Bailey said, undeterred by her cousin's short temper.

"Who do you think you are, Bailey Marie Durham Walker? Jessica Fletcher?" Tyra asked, referring to the fictional writer and sleuth portrayed by Angela Lansbury in the *Murder, She Wrote* television series.

Bailey glared at her cousin. "Jessica Fletcher doesn't cook."

"I'm referring to the way you portray yourself as a private investigator."

"Jessica Fletcher doesn't do that. She just happens to be in the wrong place at the right time. Because she writes murder mysteries, and because she works closely with police, she makes a credible witness and amateur detective."

"God, you make me sick," Tyra said, "and believe me when I tell you this, because I mean every word. It just kills me the way you go around acting like butter won't melt in your mouth."

"Such a cliché and so untrue," Bailey said. "I'm as scared as everybody else. I want to go home and turn back the clock to a time when Uncle Fred was alive, but I can't do that, Tyra. I can't go back to a gentler, better time because there wasn't one for this family. The Durhams never got along in the first place, and with Uncle Fred murdered the way he was, by his own kin, I know any chance of happiness we might have had is lost forever."

"Oh, you holier-than-thou b—"

"Give me a break," Bailey said. She tried not to blow her cool but it was far too late for polite conversation. "Even you aren't so shallow and stupid as to start a fight with me with the police so close at hand."

"Scared?"

Bailey threw Tyra an oh-please look. "Not of you."

"I could be the killer."

"You're too sloppy to be the killer, Tyra. I see that now. Thank you."

Even though it was unreasonable, Tyra was appalled. "So, you're gonna cross me off your list. Just like that?"

"Yes. But instead of feeling honored and pleased I've dropped your name off the short list of suspects, you're pissed off. Like I was saying, Tyra, you're too sloppy to pull off two sophisticated murders."

Tyra huffed and puffed as if she were running up hill. "You call a rolling pin and a blow-dryer sophisticated ways of killing people?"

Bailey huffed and puffed right back. "Sometimes, Tyra, less is more. You've heard that saying, haven't you?"

"Stick it, Bailey. I could take it to mean you're so simple nobody would think of a Goody Two-shoes like you as killing your family."

"My reputation isn't spotless, Tyra, but it is clean. How about yours?"

"I hate the way you act so superior. How can you be superior when you've left your children at home during a crisis like this?"

"Get real," Bailey said. "How could I bring them into a mess like this?"

"If I had children," Tyra said, all her bravado falling away in a neurotic rush, "I'd want them with me no matter what."

Bailey softened. "Hey, I love my girls, and I've kept them in the safest place I know, with Sam's parents."

Tyra had never had a close relationship with her own mother, a woman who abandoned her to tour France on a dirt bike only to never come back. In response to that neglect, Tyra took what she wanted when she wanted it, even if what she wanted belonged to someone else. At the moment, she wanted Bailey's self-control; Tyra had always thought Bailey's Achilles' heel was her children, but she thought now that she might be wrong.

"So," Tyra said, "it's that hunk of a husband of yours that you love more than you love your children."

Bailey was clearly disgusted. "I have no idea what you're driving at Tyra but I wish you'd get on with it."

"I've been wondering about the wild card in all this commotion."

Bailey rolled her eyes. "You mean, all this killing, don't you?"

Tyra ignored the correction. "The wild card is Sam. I've been thinking, between sips of Uncle Fred's tequila, that Sam might be unhappy with his job and ready to start his own business."

"Doing what?"

"Electronics, of course."

"Go on." Bailey's tone was patronizing, but her eyes were livid with anger.

"Sam is of the age where men want to work for themselves instead of 'the man.' Sam strikes me as that kind of a guy. I mean, he wouldn't be content to help you with your business by joining it full-time. He's too manly to be a caterer."

"You're so ignorant, Tyra. There are men who make excellent cooks, restaurant owners, and caterers."

"Some men. We agree on the phrase, this time, cousin. Some men do, but not yours. He's too high-powered, too technical for that type of work."

"Give me a break, Tyra. Sam helps me all the time."

"In a strictly lift-and-carry mode. Sam doesn't cook, does he?"

"No."

"He manages millions of dollars for a company

that downsized three times in the last eighteen months, doesn't he?"

"That's true, but how do you know this, Tyra?"

"I read the business papers. At the moment, I'm glad I kept up with the whereabouts of the relatives."

"A simple phone call would have sufficed."

Tyra snorted. "Too personal."

"Let me get this straight," Bailey said. "You think I knew Uncle Fred made me the sole beneficiary of his estate. You think I wanted to speed up his death so my husband could take control over his business, which would give Sam the means to start his own electronics company."

"That's exactly what I'm saying."

"No wonder you never married," Bailey said. "No man would be crazy enough to take you on."

Tyra's anger was back in a flash. She launched herself at her cousin.

Bailey sidestepped.

Both women crouched like boxers.

Before either could strike, Sam entered the room. He had been in the dining room talking to Dexter. He shoved Bailey to the side so that he stood between her and Tyra.

Dexter, right on Sam's heels, hooted with laughter. "Touching scene, sweet cousins," he said.

The women snarled at him.

To Sam, Dexter said, "Ever the knight in shining armor."

Sam ignored the pretty boy to attend to his wife. "Bailey, you all right?"

Disgusted, she snorted like a horse. "I can't take this anymore. Let's get outta here, Sam. Now."

"You can't," Dexter said. "Two deaths in one week in the same house is a bit too much for Hark to ignore. He can't let you go any more than he can let me go. He's too close to retirement to loosen his grip on any of us. Even if Fred's death was a suicide, Sybil's was not."

"I've been thinking about Hark's involvement in this whole thing," Tyra said. "He could have killed Fred because he's pissed off about being left out of the will, or because he wanted a sensational case to solve on his way out of the retirement door. Spite and fame."

Dexter stared at Tyra as if he saw her clearly for the first time. "You aren't an airhead after all."

Tyra grabbed a red delicious apple from the fruit bowl on the kitchen counter. She threw it at him. Dexter caught the fruit easily in his fist, polished the apple on his sleeve, then took a bite. "I'm too old," he said, "to have a food fight."

Tyra picked up a second apple, but before she could toss it at Dexter, Sam grabbed her wrist. "I think you took a swing at Sybil with the rolling pin," he said.

Tyra stilled every muscle, every thought. Her next move shocked them all: She laughed, a sound so hysterical it raised the flesh on Bailey's arms. Instinctively, Bailey went to her cousin, as if to help her in some way. "Tyra," she said, "let's go to the parlor and sit down."

"Then what, Bailey Marie, you'll soothe away my fears with homemade biscuits and orange spice tea?"

Bailey led Tyra to a chair at the desk in the kitchen and wrapped her in the kind brace of her arms. "You remember."

"Of course I remember," Tyra said. "The one time I came to your house, I was so envious of the way you soothed away your daughters' tears with tea and biscuits that I . . . I always wished you would do the same for me."

"I'll make the biscuits," Bailey said. "You make the tea."

Tyra wiped away her tears. "I'm sorry for attacking you. I'm just . . . scared."

"So am I," Bailey said. "So am I."

While Tyra went off to tidy herself up, Bailey whipped up a simple batch of buttermilk scones. She eyed her husband. "You'd think the kitchen would be off-limits. I'm glad it isn't. I know it's weird, but it's kind of like we're all under quarantine."

Sam had a one-track mind. "First Tyra was against you, now she's asking for biscuits and tea. I don't trust her."

"We've got to whittle down suspects somehow. I think that by Tyra asking for biscuits and tea, she's saying she doesn't really think I'm guilty."

"What about her theories on why you could have done it?"

"I think she was letting me know that if I did kill Uncle Fred, that was the only reason she could think of for me doing it. It's too long and wild a shot in the dark to be a viable motive for murder."

"She said something incriminating about Hark Bittersweet."

"Same thing," Bailey said. "She thinks of us and Bittersweet as authority figures. Investigators. She stated we had motive, we had opportunity, but by asking for quiet time together, she's also showing us she's not truly intimidated by us."

"She might just want to keep us in sight," Sam said. He searched the cupboards for a medium-sized mixing bowl and a nest of metal measuring cups. He found a sturdy silver stirring spoon and a set of matching measuring utensils in a drawer.

"That too," Bailey said as she quickly gathered the ingredients: all-purpose flour, sugar, salt, baking soda, baking powder, butter, buttermilk, an egg, vanilla extract, and golden raisins. "She struck a nerve when she brought up the girls though. But if I really think about it, I've been kidding myself. The girls have been in danger all along. No one in this family is safe."

"That's just it," Sam said. "The killer can't win. At this rate, only the killer will remain."

"Maybe that's the point," Bailey said, "to be the last man standing. That way, nobody wins. Nobody gets Fred's money."

EIGHTEEN

By the time Bailey got around to drinking her tea, it was already lukewarm. She downed half the cup before she realized there was something wrong. "God," she said, "this is weird."

Sam raised a brow in concern. He was nibbling a biscuit slathered in pure butter. "What do you mean, weird?"

Bailey grimaced. "This tea tastes funny."

"How?"

"I don't know exactly. It's just . . . off. I usually put a lot of honey in my tea before I even taste it, so I don't know precisely what the tea tasted like before I added sweetener."

"But?"

"This tea is gross."

Tyra added her own two cents. "Not mine." Still, she put her cup down on the table.

Sam took Bailey's tea. He sniffed, but like Bailey, he was unsure if something was really wrong or if his imagination was getting the best of him. "Don't drink it."

"If Tyra's tea is fine," Bailey said, "it just must be me."

Sam took the honey pot and peered inside. "I'll

show this to Bittersweet. You're the only person to use the honey, right?"

"Right."

"I'll get you some water from the kitchen tap."

"Thanks. My throat kind of . . . burns."

Tyra spoke is if she was afraid to say anything at all. "What's going on here? I'm telling you, I'm sitting here getting the willies."

"Nothing," Bailey said. "It's probably nothing."

Sam brought Bailey water in a glass he washed and rinsed before filling. She drank half the glass, slammed the tumbler down on the table, and promptly gripped its edges with both hands. "God," she said, "I think I'm gonna be sick."

Tyra put her warm, dry hand on Bailey's forehead, her cheek, her neck. "I hate to tell you this, but your skin feels a little cool and kind of clammy."

"Bailey?" Sam said. "You all right?"

She hunched her back and crossed her arms over her stomach. "Sam?" she said, more than a little bewildered, "I think, I think I've been poisoned!"

"How convenient," Phoebe said in the parlor, several hours after Bailey had been to the local emergency room and back with Sam, Tyra, and Detective Bittersweet. "I come out of my bedroom to have tea, and the heroine in our messed-up family drama is drugged, presumably by someone in this room. I think she did it to her own damn self."

"I didn't make the tea," Bailey said. "Tyra made the tea."

Tyra looked as if she was unsure whether she would laugh or cry. "I also went around telling everybody to meet us in the parlor, but that doesn't mean I tried to kill you."

"It's the same kind of in-your-face killing that's been going on all along," Sam said. He looked around, his eyes mean and nasty. "One of you is guilty. One of you will pay for what you've done to my wife."

"Be careful," Hark Bittersweet said. He had been summoned by Dexter as soon as Bailey became ill. "What you're saying could be construed as a threat."

"It is a threat," Sam said to the detective. "I mean what I say."

"Arrest him, Officer," Phoebe said. "The rest of our lives are at stake." Her attempt at humor in a humorless situation gained her no brownie points.

"Go back to that cave you call a bedroom and climb back in your bottle," Tyra said. "I'm innocent. So is Bailey. Sam is only protecting his wife."

"Pick a side," Phoebe said to Tyra, "and stay on it. You're making me dizzy."

Sam's fists were clinched. "We can find out what poison was used and trace it to the source."

"That could take weeks if the drug is uncommon, but my guess is that somebody used arsenic to make Bailey sick," the detective said. "I discussed it with the emergency room physician as a possibility. He said the symptoms for arsenic poisoning were definitely there. Fortunately, he was able to treat Bailey effectively without any significant side effects. She feels bad now, but she'll continue to get better."

"I trust you'll find a way to get the tea tested quickly," Sam said as calmly as he could. He was badly shaken. "You won't want someone else to bust this case before you retire, and I don't want to start busting heads around here to get the answers we need. Bittersweet, you're a couple of days down and counting."

"The clock is ticking," Bailey said.

Sam nodded his head. "That's right."

"But," Tyra said, "Bailey always drinks orange spice tea. The rest of us are pretty much into stronger stuff. Eventually, she would have had tea to settle her nerves. It was just a matter of time. Since I had tea, and I'm fine, it must have been the honey that was poisoned. Bailey is the only person here who takes her tea with honey. Anyone could have poisoned the honey, including Uncle Fred's cook, Iris."

"We all know the cook didn't do it," Phoebe said.

Sam shifted his attention to her. "Why is that?"

"She isn't here and has nothing to benefit by killing Bailey. Uncle Fred took care of her the way he took care of his secretary, his housekeeper, and the rest of his trusted employees: quite well."

"She's right," Grant said. He clearly wanted to be helpful, and it showed. "We need to find out who had recent access to the kitchen."

"Bailey!" Phoebe said.

"So anxious to condemn," Hark Bittersweet said. "Forget the truth and find a scapegoat, is that it?"

"Whatever," Phoebe said. "I just don't want to die. All this silence and secrecy within the family is making me nuts. I can't take it anymore, and what's up with that unrelenting fog out there? I feel like we're in a bad B movie or something."

"Out of everyone," Dexter said, "Bailey has had the most access to the kitchen. Open access is in keeping with the up-close-and-personal aspect of both murders and the murder attempt."

"For once," Sam said, his calm voice at odds with the murderous glint in his eyes, "I agree with you. We're forgetting to keep this simple."

"I might add," Hark Bittersweet said, "that all the silence and secrecy in this family only makes the resolution of the problem worse."

Sam had a snarl on his face, as if he wished he had the power to arrest the entire Durham clan himself. "We aren't any closer to solving Fred's murder than we were when fingers first started pointing at Bailey for the crime. Why is everyone so determined to make her the fall guy for everything that goes wrong? Is there a conspiracy at work here?"

"Huh," Phoebe said, her face full of mischief, "we don't get along well enough to form a conspiracy."

"There is the money angle," the detective said, "or rather, the lack of money and the mutual feelings of anger."

"You mean rage," Dexter said.

"I agree with Sam," Bailey said, her wits and common sense bound tight for the moment. "It's possible that more than one person is the villain here. With Detective Bittersweet so close to retirement, we're desperate for answers."

"Retirement?" Grant said, his voice ending on a high note. He turned to face the detective, who returned his stare with one of near disinterest. It was rarely easy to read Hark Bittersweet, and this occasion was no exception. "What's this about Hark?"

"I'm ready to smell the roses." This was said with only a ghost of a smile.

"Bull," Dexter said. "I don't believe you."

Bailey looked at him the same way she would look at a spider on the wall: with distaste. "Why?"

Dexter explained. "He's done little else in recent years except work as a cop and shove pet projects under Uncle Fred's nose in the hopes of getting money to finance them."

"Hey," Bailey said, "this all has to do with money. Keep that in mind, folks. The money angle applies to everyone."

"There isn't any money," Grant said.

"Yes, there is," Sam said, his confidence a volatile mix of cold-blooded arrogance and scarcely contained outrage. "Millions of it and the opportunity to gain more. I think all this killing is camouflage for the intended victim in all this madness."

Everyone stared at Bailey, who pretended she was one of the cabbage roses in the wallpaper border above the fireplace.

"Yeah," Sam said. "With Bailey dead, as well as a few extra kinfolk, Fred's money is up for grabs all over again."

"If that's the case," Bailey said, determined not to give in to cowardice by disappearing into the woodwork—or the wallpaper—"lets all meet again in the parlor at a designated hour and hold an all-night vigil or something. We'll have open discussion. All questions must be answered and no question will be taboo. Tonight, we're gonna end this thing."

"And be warned," Sam said, his eyes fixed and lacking even an ounce of subtlety. "If anything weird happens to Bailey or even looks like it's happening to Bailey, there'll be hell to pay and I'll be the man who sees that justice is carried out."

"Wait a minute," Detective Bittersweet said, "that's a threat."

Sam crushed any doubt in the detective's mind that he was merely blowing smoke. "It is, and I mean every word I said. Every one."

The detective believed him.

NINETEEN

That evening, Ridge Williams called Sam, who sat on the edge of the bed he shared with Bailey. "Phoebe was under investigation for being an accessory to the murder of one of Fred Durham's business rivals, a Craig Holland."

"Go on," Sam said.

"Holland owned a business similar to Fred's, he made trolley cars. Phoebe met Holland at a fundraising function she attended with Fred. An affair developed between the two, a rift occurred, Holland wound up dead."

"How?"

"Electrocution."

"With what?"

"An appliance in the bathtub."

"Blow-dryer?"

"Yes."

"Why did Phoebe get away with it?"

"Not enough evidence."

Sam drummed a quick tattoo with his fingers against his right kneecap. "If Craig Holland was a heavy player in Fred Durham's league, then why wasn't Phoebe's potential involvement played up more in the press? I heard about Holland's death in the news, but I didn't know the details, and I

didn't know Fred was friendly with him, let alone
that Phoebe was a murder suspect."

"Fred squashed the rumors and handled the
press. Holland's management staff helped him do
this."

"Okay," Sam said, "then presumably, Fred was
protecting Phoebe or probably more correctly, he
was protecting the Durham name and business,
just as Craig Holland's people were protecting his
name and business."

"Phoebe was never formally charged or arrested.
She had excellent lawyers. One in particular will
interest you."

"Who?"

"Grant."

Sam was surprised, and it showed in his voice.
"He has a law degree?"

"Apparently. He lived elsewhere for a time,
dropped out of sight and out of the family for a
while. The main thing you need to know is that
he studied law and has a license to practice law in
Minnesota and in California."

"Minnesota!"

"Yeah. He attended a prominent university there.
Phoebe's brush with murder brought Grant back
into the family fold. He returned to San Francisco
to represent Phoebe in an out-of-court settlement
and ended up staying."

"He doesn't practice law any longer, does he?"

"Not officially, no."

"What do you mean by 'not officially'?" Sam
said.

"He doesn't have an office but his license to
practice law is in order, both here and in Minnesota. Grant is actually a wonder boy, extremely
high IQ, voted most likely to succeed in business

while still in high school. He uses his legal knowledge to negotiate shady deals with business associates."

Sam's brain sped away at new possibilities. "Shady?"

"Ethically correct but morally corrupt."

"Huh," Sam said, "something along the lines of stealing candy from babies without getting caught?"

"Exactly," Ridge said. "Grant has scams running from Minnesota to San Francisco. Apparently, he gets his partners with the fine print in his contracts. I've never met the man but my sources tell me he's charismatic, cult leader style charismatic."

Sam nodded in silent agreement. "The kind of guy who leads ordinary people into extraordinary situations."

"Including murder," Ridge said.

"Don't tell me," Sam said, a slight twist of distaste on his lips. "Grant was involved with the death of a business associate."

"Circumstantially of course."

"And Fred kept it on the down-low."

"Way down. I could hardly find a trail between Grant and Fred, but there is a trail. No formal charges were pressed against Grant. Grant's victim was a struggling engineer who designed electronic gadgets. Grant handled copyright documentation for the deceased, a man who claimed he actually designed the electronic device that Grant later sold to a manufacturing firm for a hefty price."

Sam said, "Sounds a little like *The List* by Steve Martini."

"Never heard of it."

"Bailey read the book and told me about it. It's a story about the publishing industry. One of the main characters, a lawyer, was given the task of handling the copyright documentation for a writer who wanted to remain anonymous but wanted to receive payment for the work she created, which turned out to be a blockbuster novel. The lawyer copyrighted the work in his own name. Alter publishing industry to read electronic industry and you'll see what I mean. There is a betrayal of trust involved here, the kind that breaches ethics and reaches into the moral fiber."

"Moral fiber?" Ridge said.

Sam laughed. "All this cloak-and-dagger stuff is getting to me. I feel like Bailey and I are stranded on an island."

"Indian Island in Agatha Christie's book, *Ten Little Indians.*" Ridge's wife, Vancy, was good friends with Bailey. Both women enjoyed trading paperbacks and sharing the most interesting plots with their husbands.

"Yeah," Sam said. "One by one, the characters die." Like Ridge, Sam was thankful he had listened to his wife ramble about books. It helped him think along the lines of a murder mystery novel, all dangerous and sinister.

"Get out of the house, Sam. Get out of the city."

"I can't."

"Why?"

Sam blew a long sigh of frustration. "We're close to solving this thing. It's someone so benign that even Bailey can't figure out who it is. Her antennae just aren't up and I'm worried that if we go home, she'll open the door to a familiar face and wind up dead on the doorstep. I couldn't live with myself then, Ridge, not even for the girls."

"Don't say that."

"It's my job and my right to protect my wife. She was poisoned while I was sitting right in front of her, Ridge. As it is, I'm afraid to go to sleep right now."

"Where is she?"

"In the bathtub with the door open so I can hear her."

Ridge spoke in earnest. "Get some rest, Sam."

"That's impossible."

"Try. By not thinking about every single obstacle every waking moment, you'll give yourself the space you need to relax for a minute. You might even piece together some fact you at first thought was trivial. Go back to the beginning."

Abruptly, Sam stopped beating his fingers against his knee. Perhaps, he thought, the best clue of all had been the first piece to the puzzle. "The beginning?"

"Yeah."

"In the beginning," Sam said, "there was a note."

TWENTY

Refreshed from her bath, Bailey joined Sam at a table in their borrowed suite. In her hands was the original invitation from Fred Durham. It read:

> *Bailey my dear,*
> *I'd love for you and Sam to join me for dinner and a brief stay at the Painted Lady on Dark Hill. I encourage you to leave the girls and come alone for a quiet getaway. Call and confirm.*
> *Your loving uncle, Fred.*

"I don't see anything sinister in this invitation," Bailey said, "do you?"

"No."

Sam said, "During your telephone conversation, he hinted at having something important to tell you. Perhaps it was about leaving his fortunes to you. He said you're worth more than a million.

"His doctor bills confirm how much his cancer treatments were costing him, even with insurance. Remember, he no longer owned the carriage business and was essentially living on a fixed income, large, but fixed."

Bailey said, "And where did you run across medical records, of all things?"

"I did some snooping on my own. I figured there had to be a reason for all this madness, and so I started looking for anything obvious, something that has been staring us in the face since we got here."

Bailey positioned herself on her knees behind Sam as he sat on the bed's edge, his feet on the floor. She massaged his temples, his head, his neck. She pressed a kiss against the lower lobe of his ear and tickled him with her breath. "Talking to Ridge sure fired you up."

Sam pressed himself into the softness of Bailey's body. She felt good against his back. "It did."

"You couldn't have had much time for snooping, alone, that is, because we've been together almost exclusively since Uncle Fred's death."

"I did it after I hung up the phone with Ridge just now, while you were getting dressed after your bath."

"You'll have to explain this for me."

"The note takes us back to the beginning of all the drama. Thinking of beginnings reminded me that when we arrived in this suite, we wondered why our accommodations were changed for the first time. Whenever we've stayed here, our suite was on the first floor. This time, our suite is on the second floor, two doors away from Fred's suite. Everyone else is in another wing."

Bailey stopped her massage, her head cocked to one side. "You think Uncle Fred set me up."

"I do. I think he knew he was going to die. He had cancer, Bailey. My guess is that he wasn't getting any better. I think he staged his own death and figured you'd be the person who'd find him. I think he wanted people to believe he was murdered."

"He couldn't be sure I'd find his body."

"He based his assumptions on logical thinking."

"I follow you," Bailey said, as she resumed her massage, this time working the kinks out of his shoulders. "The maid and secretary were gone. The other relatives were in a separate wing from ours and not on the best of terms with him anyway. He figured that I would check on him out of concern. That would explain why the suite and bathroom doors were unlocked. He wanted me to have easy access."

"I agree."

"Was his business in the red or the black?"

"Ridge says he was definitely in the black."

"So why the suicide nonsense?"

"There might be a note around here explaining it all, which is why I set about looking for clues in this bedroom. I found a box of papers, Bailey, medical records included."

"Okay, so you still think there's a note for me somewhere explaining all this mess."

Sam lifted Bailey's hands from his shoulders, then kissed the insides of her palms. "I do."

Bailey sighed, her heart a heavy weight in her chest. "I think we should look in the kitchen. Every time I come to the Painted Lady, I bake a chocolate delight cake for Uncle Fred. His regular cook is allergic to chocolate, so she doesn't make chocolate dishes. If there's a note for me, my guess is that it's in the box of cocoa I'd use to make the batter for the cake."

"You scare me sometimes, Bailey."

"I'm a Durham, Sam. A little crazy runs in all of us. I'm no exception. Let's check out the cocoa. It should be on the third shelf in the kitchen pantry."

It was.

With shaking fingers, Bailey pulled the note from the cocoa box, shook off the chocolate, and leaned heavily against her husband. She cleared her throat once, twice, before saying out loud:

Bailey my dear,

Please forgive this selfish old man his final flight of fancy. If you've found this little letter, then you'll also know that I've left the Durham fortune to you and to Sam. As you can see, I've chosen well: You found this letter and solved the mystery of my death. Your finding this letter proves my theory that none of the others in our clan were fitting of the throne I left behind. I wanted to prove your superior talents as compared to your cousins.

By now, you've uncovered the past scams and murders committed by your cousins. Your own life has been tainted with murder but your saving grace in those deaths was the fact that you and your husband worked together to solve those murder mysteries. By solving those mysteries you brought justice to the deceased. That's all I want, Bailey: justice.

What is justice? It is truth, integrity, and fairness, all the attributes both your enemies and your friends can accurately apply to you. It is you, Bailey, who deserves to carry on the family name with honor.

But first, I must explain why I chose you, my dear. Over the years, I watched you from a distance, via Hark Bittersweet. I trust that he's been very helpful to you in your current investigation of my death. And yes, my dear, I did kill myself.

Rather me than the cancer or those drugs and other therapy prescribed by the best physicians the city has to offer. Quite simply, my dear, I grew tired of living and wanted to go out with a bit of, what shall I say? Flare. We Durhams were never known for our modesty, including you, my dear nosy Bailey Marie. Only you would have thought to check the cocoa box for a secret hiding place. As I said, you are definitely superior, prime Durham stock.

Extreme wealth is a great comfort. Use what I've given you to aid your family, your friends, and your community as you see fit. Don't let my money go to waste and don't throw it away because of my shenanigans. Without my violent death, you might never have known the full depth of your cousins' treachery, sins past and sins present. As sure as I am of you, I'm even more sure of them. They abused my kindness in life, I abused them in death. I am at peace my dear, for once in my life, true peace.

As anyone born into money, I've developed an air of indifference about it. As one nourished by true love, Sam's love for you and your love for him, you've developed an air of indifference about anything beyond your nuclear family unit. Perhaps, somewhere in the middle, is a defining point of grace for us both. Take the money, Bailey. Do what I couldn't do in life: give from the heart.

Your loving uncle, Fred Durham

P.S. I'm sure Sam will want this note authenticated. Based on modern forensic science, this task should be easily and successfully accomplished. This is why I wrote you alone an invitation, using the same pen and paper as I've used to write this note. Both pen and paper are in the safety deposit box at the bank at the foot of Dark Hill, the one with the angels carved above the front door. You are my angel, Bailey, this old man's salvation.

Bailey put the note and the box of cocoa in a large plastic freezer bag. "Well, Sam, I guess the only thing left to do is to meet the rest of the family for the last revelation, the identity of the true killer among us."

"You think you know who it is?"

"Yes."

Sam pulled his wife into his arms and pressed her cheek against his chest. "When did you figure it out?"

"In the bathtub."

"While I was talking to Ridge on the phone?"

"Yep."

"Tell me, baby, whodunit?"

After she whispered her secret in his ear, Sam said, "We'll need a tape recorder and backup."

"You make those arrangements with Hark Bittersweet while I summon the family together for the last hurrah. It's only fitting that we meet in the parlor; it's everybody's stomping ground."

TWENTY-ONE

At the designated time that evening, 7:00 P.M., the relatives and Detective Bittersweet assembled in the parlor. Outside, the city of San Francisco was bright and cloudless, the temperature seventy-three degrees, the warmest day of the week.

To celebrate the beautiful day, residents on Dark Hill washed their cars, played with their children on postage stamp–sized lawns, strolled arm in arm through the neighborhood, and, for the most part, were successful in pretending there were no police officers loitering about the manicured grounds of the Painted Lady.

The mood inside the parlor was inquisitive, all arguments put briefly on hold as each occupant assessed the other for telltale signs of guilt. Various versions of secrecy appeared in the relatives' body language:

Tyra had a hard time focusing on any one person in particular. She toyed with the gold hoop dangling from her left ear with a finger whose nail was marred with chipped red polish.

Dexter appeared mildly amused, though the smile he wore was almost entirely artificial and somewhat belligerent as he leaned his hip against the wall near the window, his physically fit body clearly defined in the gray-on-gray outfit he had chosen to wear, a casual look that stood out against the dark paper on the parlor walls.

Grant simply could not keep still. He kept rubbing his hands together, often sliding them over his stonewashed jeans, and either fingering the gunmetal-colored watch at his wrist or wrapping his palm around the back of his own thick neck, as if the collar of his shirt was driving him to the very edge of distraction.

Phoebe, dressed in a camel-colored shift that used her body to shape the dress, kept cutting her eyes at everyone, even though she looked no one directly in the face. Like Dexter, she remained standing, near the wet bar, her arms crossed, her fingers digging into the flesh of her forearms.

Detective Bittersweet stood in front of the fireplace, its grate empty, his bearing proud and direct, as if he had nothing to hide. In fact, he appeared smug, his tie loose about his neck, his casual suit jacket as open as the expression on his face. He projected the image of a man ready to retire with the most sensational case of his career all wound expertly tight and sweet for the prosecution.

Bailey and Sam sat together on one of the sofas, Hark Bittersweet behind them, his relaxed presence at their back speaking in loud volumes to the family members at large. His position behind the Walkers showed the family that the trio had finally reached a point of trust, a point that allowed them to function as allies.

Touching Sam lightly on the arm, in an unconscious quest for comfort and reassurance from the man she loved, Bailey gathered the courage to be the first person to speak. "In spite of so many events moving so quickly this week, Sam and I figured out what happened to Uncle Fred and to Sybil."

Phoebe looked as if she was barely able to control the frustration that simmered just below her surface facade. Her nostrils were flared, her eyes were round, her body as taut as the strings on a very rare, very expensive violin. "This is ridiculous," she said, her pronunciation close to a hiss. "Hark ought to be the one calling the shots in here tonight, not you, Bailey Marie." Phoebe paused to glare at Sam. "You either."

As if her nervous energy was too intense to contain, Tyra flung her hands in the air. She stamped the heel of her right leather sandal against the Turkish rug on the hardwood floor, her recent camaraderie with Bailey over biscuits and tea marred by her cousin's terrible episode with poison.

It was clear to everyone that Tyra was not sure whom to trust, let alone whom to side with in the darkening parlor. She flicked on a table lamp, as if the glow of false light might warm her skin. "This is just too damned much, that's what it is. Too. Damned. Much."

Grant flexed his shoulders and rocked his neck to the side until the vertebrae cracked, even the skin on his face looked tight enough to crack. "Before we start throwing blows at one another," he said, "I'm heading for Fred's bourbon—if there's any left—in honor of Sybil."

"Same here," Dexter said. To the detective he added, "From the amount of patrol cars you've got outside, I imagine you're sending a message to the killer that the only way out of this place is through a blaze of bullets."

The detective bowed his head, slightly, as if in

humility; however, his tone was a shade too mocking. "Just doing my job."

Phoebe let out a snarl that was half spit, half vicious growl. She had known the detective too long to be buffaloed by his bogus humble attitude. He might want everybody to forget it, but he, too, had stood to inherit from Fred's original will. "Of all the nerve," she said, her voice low and cold enough to carry a windchill factor.

Bailey eyeballed Phoebe with open disdain. "Yes. Nerve. We'll get to that in a minute, so save the pit bull act."

Phoebe's body angled itself toward Bailey as if she might jump at her from across the room, throw her to the Turkish rug, and beat the daylights out of her; however, Dexter's hand on Phoebe's shoulder kept her firmly in place. He had a grip like heavy metal.

Bailey forced herself to continue. She said, "First of all, there's a real psycho in this room, somebody who is very human and ordinary on the outside, but seething with anger on the inside."

"Seething?" Grant said, his brows hiked to the max. "Don't you think you're being a bit too melodramatic?"

Sam's command was softly spoken. "Quiet."

Bailey drew strength from the positive energy thrown around her by Sam's love. His love pressed down on her face and body like warm hands, it blew into her lungs like the barest whisper of smoke.

"Let's face it," she said, "we've all been jerks at some point or another during the big fat mess we've been dealing with this week, which also made it hard to detect the true villain among us. We all had the same motives, the same opportunities, the same benefits, but only one of us was so outraged that murder became a viable option."

Tyra looked at her cousin with respect; still, hers was not simply a pretty face, as her features were distorted by paranoia. "Bailey," she said, "you've got balls."

Bailey smiled self-consciously. "Thank you."

Phoebe jumped up, her eyes wild, her hair knocked out of order by her own jittery fingers. "No! I won't listen to you. None of us will. Let Hark do the talking. He's the real police."

Sam couldn't care less about all the rapid-fire feelings careening through the well-dressed occupants in the well-dressed room. When it got down to the wire, he felt heartless when it came to anyone's pain and suffering other than his wife's; Bailey was the only person in the parlor, other than himself and the detective, with any true self-control.

Silently vowing to keep order in the parlor, Sam pointed to Phoebe and said with all the deliberate menace he could muster, "Sit."

Livid, Phoebe threw her drink at him. When three cubes of ice hit her feet, she drop-kicked the ice across the room. "Sit, my ass. I don't answer to you."

Detective Bittersweet dangled a pair of handcuffs in Phoebe's line of vision. He said nothing, but Dexter did. "Cuffs won't be necessary," he said. To Phoebe, he added, "Put a lid on it, cuz. You're blowing it for the rest of us. I want to know what happened to Sybil and Fred. We all do."

Once Phoebe was back in her chair, Sam said to Bailey, "Shoot."

Dressed in a navy pantsuit trimmed in white, she looked like a lawyer in a television courtroom

drama. "First of all," Bailey said, "there were two
wills. The old one left every surviving Durham, including my adoptive sister, an equal share of Fred's
estate. In this will, according to Malinder Simmons,
all Fred's assets were supposed to be liquidated. In
the second and final will, he left everything to me,
intact, unliquidated."

Sam added his two cents' worth of commentary.
"Some of you knew about the final will for sure,
but most only suspected the truth. I thought it was
rude to bring it up the first night we all gathered
for dinner, but then I finally realized that it's the
will that enticed you all to come to the Painted
Lady in the first place, this, when you clearly can't
stand one another. You were after the facts, the
truth, but only as the truth related to your private
lives. For whatever spiteful reason, Fred dangled
the will in front of you like the proverbial carrot.
In this way, he was as conniving and back-stabbing
as you are."

Grant cracked his neck again. "What do you
have to say about this, Hark?"

The detective answered the question without
missing a beat. "I say everyone showed up to hear
about the new will from Fred, just as Bailey said,
only he never mentioned it. I say that each of you
came to the Painted Lady prepared to fight with
Fred for your financial lives, only you never got a
chance to fight for your lives because he lost his
own the next morning."

Hark ran his eyes over each person in the room,
then said, "Let's face it, living in San Francisco
right now is expensive and getting more expensive
all the time. Either you're rich and getting richer
or poor and getting poorer. You guys needed the
original will to stay intact, so you hung around all

week to find out if the second will was void for
any reason and to find out for yourselves if Fred
was killed or if Fred killed himself."

"Except for Bailey, of course," Dexter said.
"Bailey was the only one left in the dark, if we are
to believe her side of the story, that is."

"Believe it," the detective said. "Fred left de-
tailed papers with his attorneys about who knew
what and when. He wanted Bailey to represent him
after his death. We all know how careful he was
as a businessman. He knew what he was doing, so
his death in the bathtub was not accidental, nor
was it a sudden decision."

Dexter made a faint *tsk* sound of disbelief. He
actually appeared to be shell-shocked. "So, he really did do it. He really did commit suicide." Dexter spoke more to himself than to anyone else and
kept shaking his head while he said it.

Bailey hated to admit the sad and sorry truth.
"Yes, he did."

Tyra was clearly bewildered and cared nothing
about anyone else's opinion of her at the moment.
She spoke to Hark Bittersweet. "But you said he
was murdered. There weren't any fingerprints on
the blow-dryer, remember? You said so yourself."

Hark Bittersweet was so coldly professional, so
set on smooth, Sam and Bailey had to remind
themselves he was on their side; he might have
been discussing flight schedules with United Air-
lines for all the spark he injected into his voice.
"I did."

Tyra kept talking, as if there had been no interruption in her conversational flow. She made random gestures with her hands, as if unsure about
what to do with them. "Now, you're saying it's suicide. Trouble is, you sounded so final before, like

you really knew what you were talking about. You're a cop, for crying out loud. Make up your mind one way or the other. Please."

"Think of it this way," Bailey said, "Fred's death was about control. He was dying of cancer. He was refusing all intensive forms of therapy because he was old and because he wasn't willing to accept the harsh side effects associated with the treatment plan proposed by his doctors. He knew he was going to die, and so he decided to do it his way, on his own time."

Tyra jumped into the middle of Bailey's explanation. "Selfish old bastard. He knew we would fight over the money."

"And you did," Sam said.

"He set us up," Grant said.

Detective Bittersweet recrossed his legs before he spoke. "Your uncle was a wise, if unorthodox man until the end. Fred set you up to prove only one of the surviving Durhams is worthy of the changes he made in the second will."

"Bailey." Tyra said her cousin's name like an epithet.

Sam's expression was that of an extremely large, extremely fit cat, a jungle cat. Sam's muscles were bunched and primed to spring into action with very little provocation; Bailey had always been the guiding light in this family drama, and he was determined to keep that light shining full into everybody's face.

"Yes. Bailey," he said with pride. "She has never wanted anything other than justice for Fred. While the rest of you worried about your cut from his estate, Bailey was worried one of you might have done him in for personal gain. The idea of it made her sick."

"Give me a break," Phoebe said. "We were all worried."

"That's true," Grant said. "We were right, too, to be worried, that is. After all, somebody whacked Sybil. Just because we're afraid to talk about it, doesn't mean we can sweep her death under the rug. Who did it, Hark? Who killed, Sybil?"

"I'd say your guess is better than mine. You tell me," the detective said. He continued to fiddle around with the handcuffs.

Tyra jumped up, high, as if something had stung her on the behind. "I'm getting the flip outta here."

"Nobody leaves," Sam said. "Nobody."

"Who died and left you in charge?" Tyra said. "But I guess that's a stupid question, isn't it? Fred died and when he died, he left you in charge of every damn thing. You and Miss High and Dog-gone Mighty."

"That's right," Sam said. He left out the *and don't you forget it* part, but everyone present got the right implication from his tone of voice; his patience had worn clean through.

Authority deepened the detective's voice. "That's not why you can't leave. You can't leave because I've got cops posted at every exit. Keep that in mind . . . all of you. Nobody leaves until I say so."

"Of course," Grant said. "We don't want a circus show for the street gawkers."

"Okay, cuz," Dexter said to Bailey, "whodunit?"

Bailey looked as if she had reached the end of the world as she knew it, but she also recognized that it was time to name names and take prisoners, so she did exactly that when she said, "Phoebe."

The only sound in the room was heavy breathing: Phoebe's.

Dexter cocked his head to the side, the lines in his forehead stacked in a frown. "I don't get it. Phoebe?"

Bailey turned to Sam. "Go ahead. Tell 'em."

"Gladly. Since the beginning, Bailey and I have been dealing with an outside investigator, a homicide detective named Ridge Williams, who discovered Phoebe's past encounter with murder."

Grant cleared his throat. Twice. "She was acquitted."

"Barely," Hark Bittersweet said, "just barely." The last two words were directed at Phoebe who held herself at some type of emotional distance, her manner resembling, to him, a woman mesmerized by the antics of acrobats in a live stage performance. Perhaps, he mused, she was waiting for a curtain call.

"Tell me something, Hark," Dexter said, "how is it that Sam and Bailey figured all this out and not you? That Phoebe had a run-in with . . . murder before? And what kind of murder was it?"

Hark explained the same facts Ridge had provided Sam and Bailey over the telephone, the same facts he and the Walkers had gone over together prior to this final gathering in the parlor.

He said, "Phoebe's escapade occurred while I was going through a rather nasty divorce with my wife. I wasn't in the homicide division at that time, which made it easier for Fred and Grant to hush things up."

"Bull," Tyra said. "You had to have known."

Dexter swung his eyes at her. He spoke low, his face open and earnest as he implored Tyra to tell him the truth. "Did you?"

Tyra was the first to break contact. "No."

"Neither did I."

"Okay," she said, "so it's possible. Come to think of it, your ex-wife was a real bitch. I remember she totally emptied your house before your divorce and just barely left you some paint on the walls. I heard she even stripped the wallpaper in one room."

The detective wore a pained expression. "Let's get back to Phoebe."

Phoebe suddenly laughed, the sound wild and desperate with just enough delight thrown in to give everybody in the parlor the creeps.

Tyra, her chipped nail polish slowly but surely being gnawed away, shivered as if the air had suddenly dropped six degrees. "She's crazy. If she did it, she's crazy. Look at her, rocking and laughing and carrying on like a loon."

Bailey took up the explanation of whodunit. "My bet is that Phoebe is pretending she's crazy. I think she's already at work on an insanity defense."

Dexter crossed the room to the wet bar, grabbed the bourbon bottle by its neck with his left fist, and returned to his position by the window. He took a long, hard pull from the bottle, then wiped his mouth with the back of his right hand. "She's pretending insanity because she knows no jury is going to believe she accidentally caused someone's death with a blow-dryer a second time."

"Actually," Bailey said, "Uncle Fred really did do it. There should be no more going back and forth on that issue. He also wanted to flush out the ugly in this family, which he did. Phoebe killed Sybil when Sybil figured out she was planning to kill Uncle Fred."

"Bailey's right," Grant said. "I told Sybil about how I helped get Phoebe off the hook in Craig Holland's murder, which was ruled an accidental death. It wasn't accidental. In a fit of rage, Phoebe threw her own blow-dryer in the tub while Craig was taking a soak in her apartment. She had just washed her hair and was drying it when the two started arguing, one thing led to another, and Craig ended up dead."

"Go on," Phoebe said, "talk about me like I'm not freakin' sitting here."

"You mean to confess?" Bailey said.

Phoebe laughed again, the sound stinging and obscene. "Please. Give me a break. You people think you've got me trapped in this room and scared. Well, I'm not scared. You said yourself Uncle Fred killed himself. As for Sybil . . ."

"We got one excellent print from the baby finger on your right hand," Hark Bittersweet said.

Phoebe had the gall to smirk. "Don't forget. Sybil wrote Bailey's name on the wall, not my name."

Bailey pounced on Phoebe's slip of the tongue before the detective could get in a word. "No one ever said my name was written on the wall. When Hark first told us about Sybil's murder, he said she wrote my name on the mirror, not the wall. I think you went back to check on Sybil to make sure she was really dead and noticed she'd written my name instead of yours. She wrote my name because she wanted me to keep digging. She knew you were guilty but if I ended up getting arrested, she also knew Sam would work doubly hard to decipher the truth, especially with my name written at the crime science in blood, kind of like the classic pointed finger. Sybil took a gamble on me and won, just like Uncle Fred."

Grant stared at Phoebe as if her skin were falling off her face. "Give it up, why don't you? Even I'm convinced."

Dexter nodded in agreement, but it was Tyra

who said, "Grant's right. Sybil was always comment-
ing that Bailey is a Goody Two-shoes. She did
mean that even though she said it sarcastically.
Face it, Phoebe, you're busted."

Phoebe's mouth stretched into a slow sinister
smile that had Bailey inching closer to Sam on the
vintage Victorian sofa.

Phoebe shrugged as if she had thrown her cares
to the wind. "All right. I did it. I figured you'd
get around to knowing it was me eventually. Truth
is, Fred wouldn't loan me money anymore, let
alone leave it to me in his will. He cut me off after
Craig's death and wouldn't even listen to me when
I asked him to help me out one more time." She
still sounded outraged.

Hark said, "You owe more than a hundred thousand dollars in credit card fees. I believe this was
your driving factor, what pushed you over the
edge."

"He could have paid them off," Phoebe said
with spite. "He should have paid them off. I told
him I'd get even with him someday, but I guess
he had the last word after all, the old bastard."

Sam asked the one question that had nagged
him repeatedly: "Why did you give Bailey enough
poison to make her sick, not kill her?"

"I couldn't be certain who would use the honey.
I hoped she would, and I wanted to scare her. I
knew she wouldn't give me any money either and
so I was mad at her too."

"I can't believe any of this," Bailey said. "It's
so . . . bizarre. With the exception of you grinning
like an idiot, having the truth come out seems . . .
flat."

"You expected guns? A knife? Rat poison? If I

was in to all that, I'd have knocked Fred off and
Sybil all in one night. One gun. Two bullets."

"When you planned to kill Fred, it was for
greed. When you killed Sybil, it was out of anger,"
Sam said.

Phoebe shrugged her shoulders once more.
"Pretty much."

"So, you admit it?" Bailey said.

"What do you think, Miss Know It All? Miss
High and Mighty? Hark's got my fingerprint on
the rolling pin."

"I certainly do," Hark said. "Come on, Phoebe,
it's time to go." He cuffed her and led her away
to a waiting police car. Two reporters sprang from
the lawn to take pictures and fire questions at
Hark and to Phoebe. Phoebe had the presence of
mind to smile for the cameras and say, "No comment."

From the dusty steps of the Painted Lady, Dexter
said, "I half expected Hark to be the killer."

"Me too," Bailey said. "He kept showing up
whenever I turned around, and it scared me. Finally, Sam and I took a chance and went to meet
him at his house. We kicked around some ideas
with him and came up with Phoebe."

Tyra shook her head. "Look at her, sitting in
the back of that cop car and smiling her stupid
head off for the cameras. Reminds me of the killer
heroine in the book *Crazy in Alabama* by Mark
Childress. Maybe Phoebe really is nuts. I mean,
maybe she's not faking just to get out of hard time
for Sybil's murder."

"There's no maybe about it," Sam said. "She
killed her lover, her cousin, and was playing
around with killing Bailey too."

Grant said, "She was afraid of you, Sam. I think

it's why she didn't do Bailey in. She didn't want to deal with you."

Sam was grim. "She was right. It was the second reason Hark stayed so close. He was afraid I'd hurt someone in defense of Bailey."

Dexter eyed Sam. "Would you have hurt her? Phoebe, I mean?"

"Physically? No, even though part of me might have wanted to hurt her in retaliation for what she did to Bailey, I would have tied her up or locked her in a room until the police got here to claim her."

"She never would have stood for that," Grant said. "She'd have hurt herself trying to get away."

"That's what we figured," Bailey said. "It's why the final parlor scene thing worked out so well. Phoebe is basically a nonviolent person with a very twisted mental screw when she gets mad."

"I guess it's true," Sam said, "murder really is terribly revealing."

TWENTY-TWO

That evening, Sam and Bailey made final arrangements to close down the Painted Lady. Fred's attorney, Malinder Simmons, was assigned the task of overseeing the sale of the mansion and the disposition of its furnishings.

At Bailey's suggestion, Malinder also hired Fred's former secretary, Joan Harrington, to assist him with the inventory and listing of every item contained within the papered walls of the Painted Lady, right down to the cloisonné doorknobs, the silver candlesticks, the pots and pans. As stipulated in Fred's second and final will, only Bailey inherited the property on Dark Hill and Fred's money. The other relatives inherited nothing.

Sam planned to open his own electronics firm, somewhere in the Silicone Valley, with Ridge Williams serving as head of his security systems. Malinder Simmons offered to assist in whatever way the men required, which included the setting up of meetings and briefings about the true depth and scope of Fred Durham's business holdings.

All final decisions about money and legal matters related to the inheritance were made by Bailey, the only Durham Fred had legally recognized. In turn,

Bailey enlisted the aid of her sister, Daphne, the woman she had been raised with since infancy.

Even though it was true that Daphne was an adopted child, and that they did not share the same Durham blood, it was also true that the two young and talented women had been raised with no distinction between them by parents who doted on them in equal, emotional proportions.

Like Malinder Simmons, Daphne was a lawyer, fully skilled professionally to support and guide her sister in whatever Bailey planned to do in the near or distant future, something Fred would have considered as he planned and carried out the last moments of his long and fruitful life. Bailey understood that by keeping Daphne out of the will, Fred had also kept her from being a target for Phoebe.

After the preliminary phone calls were made to activate the first steps of estate management, and after Tyra, Dexter, and Grant had bid their farewells, Sam and Bailey left the Painted Lady to celebrate their wedding anniversary.

They had spent a roller-coaster week on Dark Hill and were more than ready to move on, their goal to drive down Highway One, the very edge of the Pacific rim, the ocean on their right, the mountains on their left, a scattering of roadside businesses along the scenic way.

There were only a few cars on the winding road, the distances between each car stretched out so far that it seemed to Sam and Bailey that the Pacific coast, and their limitless view of its massive, life-affirming ocean, belonged solely to them.

"Last night," Bailey said, her voice a pleasant, wispy sound in the smoothly gliding sedan, "I dreamed of Italy."

"Oh, yeah?"

"Yeah."

In Bailey's dream there were palaces so grand that the romantic, soaring creations made the Painted Lady look more like a quaint potter's cottage than an expensive mansion. Instead of Victorian homes, like those on Dark Hill, or the stucco homes that dominated the Walkers' own California neighborhood, in Bailey's dream, she saw homes styled in Baroque and Arabic, saw churches with Gothic images and Byzantine designs.

In the dream, she and Sam toured the back alleys of Venice, nestled together in one fabled gondola after another, those narrow, flat-bottomed boats with the high pointed ends used to navigate the city streets, streets that were really skinny canals that flowed between the homes of millions.

Bailey had heard that the venerable city of Venice was slowly, perhaps irrevocably sinking into the water that rimmed its borders, and that the water—sinuous, ever present, and always moving—was eroding the ancient churches, revered palaces, and majestic towers.

Bailey longed to see this living museum. After spending a week in the Painted Lady, that finely restored flash from a past so checkered in American folklore and legend that it had activated her secret desire to visit Venice, the Italian city where gondoliers still sang sweet songs of love to anyone who cared to listen.

Sam took his eyes off the winding road long enough to sweep his admiring gaze over Bailey's bemused face, her extended silence prompting him to say with humor, "Venice, Italy, huh? Let's go in the spring."

Bailey opened her eyes and smiled at him. He

really was the most wonderful man she had ever known. "I wasn't hinting at a trip."

"Fred taught me something that I'll always remember: Live in the moment, with no regrets. He had a full life and so, even though his death was a tragic one, he felt at peace with himself and with his rewards in life. He only wanted the family fortune to be left in hands that wouldn't squander the legacy started by John Durham."

"I'm with you, Sam. I'm living for the moment too. I'm glad we're going on ahead with our road trip down the coast. To tell you the truth, I'm pretty much ready to go on home, but I suppose we're lucky to get a chance to regroup before we meet up with the girls again. We've crammed a lot into every day we've been away."

"I don't know how to thank my parents."

"They never had a honeymoon," Bailey said, her words slow and thoughtful. She, too, had been wondering how to reward her in-laws for their unflagging support and devotion to her, Sam, and their children.

Sam and Bailey recognized that not every married couple was as fortunate as they were when it came to extended family like Sam's parents or favored friends such as Ridge and Vancy Williams, a couple so close to the Walkers they had become family. For this reason Sam and Bailey worked diligently at not taking irreplaceable family or dear friends for granted, something easy to do during the busy days and times of their lives

It seemed to Bailey as if time moved faster than she could keep up with anymore, even with the daily planner she carried in her oversize shoulder bag. Perhaps the only way to slow time down, she reasoned, was to take a week here and there to go on vacation, and when she could not take a vacation, to at least end her day with an expression of her gratitude for the good things in life—those personal riches like having someone to love who loved you back—that money could never buy.

"Let's send your parents to Spain," she finally said. "They're always talking about going there someday."

"Great idea."

Bailey placed her hand on Sam's thigh. She knew every one of those bulging muscles and was thankful he kept himself fit by running every day that he could. "I bet you keep thinking about your own business," she said. "Even though the electronics market is very competitive right now, you've been in the game for so long, you ought to be able to find your own niche."

"I'm sure of it," Sam said. "I can hardly wait to get together with Ridge about running security for me. I need a right-hand man, and he's the best man for the job. This whole week has been incredible. When we left home, we were comfortably well off, definitely middle class, but now we've got enough money to change people's lives, to create new jobs in New Hope, to feed money into community programs that benefit music and art and science for kids, not just athletics."

"Hey, slow down, handsome. I'll be heading up the kid-related projects and one of the first things I'd like to do is set up scholarship funding. Joan Harrington said she'd consult with Daphne regarding the policies and pitfalls Fred discovered in his own work as a philanthropist. I can hardly wait to get started."

Sam nodded in agreement. "It feels strange to talk the way we're talking right now. When we left home, we had the blues about our relationship and now we're carrying on like crazy about the future. I feel as if Fred would be happy for us and that somewhere, somehow, he understands how lucky we feel. I think he'd be proud of the Fred Durham Foundation you're planning. He'd be proud you've got your sister riding shotgun with you on the project. Like Ridge will be my right hand, Daphne will be yours."

Bailey was radiant. There had been so much death and violence in one week that she was able to embrace Fred's legacy with all her heart, with all her soul, and to share this great fortune with her family and friends was tremendous. She said, "I love you, Sam."

"And I love you. Now tell me, why were you dreaming of Italy?"

"Well," Bailey said, "I've been thinking about the things we could do with all the money Fred left us. We could give half of it away and still be rich off the interest on his savings accounts. After all our bills are paid off, then what, I wondered? Travel. That ties in to living in the moment. It's kind of like being retired at an early age and seeing the world through the eyes of someone given a second chance at life, which is basically what we've got."

"You mean, as in money creating freedom?"

"Yes," Bailey said. "Fred lived a full life and he helped so many people along the way, even people undeserving, like the greedy members of my family. I want to live the same kind of life, one known more for giving than receiving. Know what I mean?"

"Yeah. Now tell me about Italy? Why not France or Russia?"

"When I think of Italy, I think of cathedrals and vineyards and fine food, of vendettas as old as the United States. I think of the characters Mario Puzo created in his Godfather books about the mystique and power of the Italian mafia, and I think of Patricia Cornwell's depiction of the forensic pathologist and lawyer, Kay Scarpetta, whose roots were connected to poor Italian immigrants."

"Bailey," Sam said, "what in the world are you talking about?"

She laughed. "The Puzo books and the Scarpetta character make me think of Italy in terms of a fantasy place, a place that's larger than life, where wild and unexpected fortune falls on ordinary people, people like us. Italy is all about beginnings and endings, about corruption and redemption—about life. I want to see it all, Sam, with you."

Sam was leaning so hard across the middle console, he was reminded of the early days in their marriage, when they could scarcely stand to be separated, even for a single moment.

Beginnings.

In their beginning there had been faith, hope, and love. Their union had become sacrosanct, a thing of beauty so cherished, it had touched the life of a failing, terminally ill man, Fred Durham, and had given him hope in his darkest hour of need, a time when his dreams for the future could only be carried on by someone savvy enough to not simply understand the value of his legacy, but to use his legacy wisely.

And so, like the gondola, a symbol of travel through the waterways of life, a vehicle basically unchanged throughout the centuries, the Durham family fortune was also a symbol of travel through the intricacies of life, an instrument of power essentially unchanged from its inception, beginning with John Durham, connecting with Fred Durham, and continuing with Bailey Marie Durham Walker.

Sam looked through the beauty of his wife's eyes, into the center of her soul, and there he found more than peace, he found satisfaction so grand there was no name to properly describe the great depth of his emotion.

Sam was so preoccupied with his wife and the crafting of their revised future together, he failed to notice they were no longer alone on the narrow, twisting coastal highway. There was a sport utility vehicle right behind them. It gained on them close and closer still.

TWENTY-THREE

Equally oblivious to the SUV behind them, Bailey admired Sam's deftness at the wheel. From her vantage point beside him in the sedan, a compact disc featuring a French guitar player in the background, she was content to simply run her gaze over his long, muscular body and to make small talk of dreams and visions for their happy future. For Bailey, Sam would always set the standard in the way she measured men in her personal and professional life.

The driver behind them bore down upon them, far too quickly to be safe in the mountains, and then, suddenly, the SUV's driver tripped a warning light in Sam's mind, a warning so strong it caused his hackles to rise.

Something was off base here, terribly off base, and Sam watched in growing consternation as the navy blue sport utility, a Ford from the mid-eighties, came so close to his rear bumper he was unable to read its license plate, and the driver, a man with a swarthy, black-bearded complexion, looked hell-bent on making both cars crash.

Bailey held on to the hard leather dash to keep her balance, a worried frown on her lovely brown face. "This can't be happening," she said over and over. "It can't."

The only thing Sam could do to reassure her was to keep the four wheels of his sedan on the road, keep them from being shoved into the mountainside, or worse, off the cliff and into the Pacific.

Angry, he estimated their chance of survival at speeds ranging from fifty-five to sixty miles per hour at the tragedy level. It took every scrap of his concentration to stay on the road, which made it impossible to spare another glance at Bailey's face: Her silence, however, spoke volumes.

"Maybe you were right," he said between clenched teeth. "Maybe there really was a conspiracy theory all along."

Bailey jammed both her feet against the floorboard. It was all she could do not to wail and moan her terror. "Drive, Sam. Drive!"

Together, Sam, Bailey, and their bearded assailant careened around a curve on two squealing wheels.

Sam spoke through clenched teeth. "I can't believe the cell phone is in the trunk with the luggage."

"I can't believe it either," she said. "We're not prepared, Sam. We're gonna die!"

Sam's face was a deadly smorgasbord of riotous feelings. If he could spare the breath, he would have cussed up a storm. If he ran into oncoming traffic, there would be no survivors, and without a witness to the crime, with Phoebe Durham in jail for killing Sybil, few people would suspect the Walkers' accident was anything suspicious.

Sam wanted to shout his frustration but the last time he had done that, he was nine years old and one of his brothers had crashed the garage door on the fingers of his left hand. The mountains and the sea would be far less merciful than the wooden garage door, which had left his hand scarred but intact. Bailey's self-control kept Sam's own courage up. If there was a way to get out of this mess alive, they would. The sedan roared ahead, the SUV right behind him.

Knick, bump, slide, squeal.
Knick, bump, slide, squeal.

Soon, Sam knew, there would be no survivors of the cat-and-mouse game they were forced to play.

Without warning, the SUV slacked off its pursuit, and if the assailant's mission had been to scare the pure daylights out of Sam and Bailey, the mission had been accomplished.

"Bailey," Sam said, "get his license plate!"

"It's covered with tape or something."

"Tape?"

"Hell, I don't know! Just drive!"

Sam stomped his foot, hard, on the gas pedal. The sedan shot forward. On the opposite side of the road was a red Trans Am, its T-top open. Had the two cars collided, there would have been only dust and metal fragments left behind; like Sam's sedan, the Trans Am was speeding.

Pop.
Pop.
Pop.

Bailey grabbed Sam's thigh, realized what she was doing, and grabbed hold of the dash instead. "Sam," she said, "he's got a gun!"

Sam uttered a long and vicious stream of epithets, but the biggest shock of all was Bailey's next outrageous statement.

"Sam," she said, "it's Hark Bittersweet!"

Sam said the "F" word. Twice.

Bailey could no longer control herself. She screamed so loud she drowned out the sound of the French guitar. "It was a trap, Sam! It was a conspiracy all along."

She was so appalled, so outdone, Bailey could scarcely take everything that was happening in to her mind at once. She and Sam had been in the detective's house. They had shared information about the crimes committed at the Painted Lady. They had trusted him, and now there he was, trying to shoot them to death—or was he warning them?

Pop.

Pop.

"I should have followed my hunch," Sam said. "I didn't trust Bittersweet from the second I laid eyes on him."

"Bullet holes," Bailey said. "If we crash and can't explain ourselves, bullet holes in the car will prove our wreck wasn't an accident. Even if we end up in the ocean . . . wait, if we end up in the ocean, we'll never be found! Step on it, Sam! Go! Go!"

He slowed down for the next curve, the SUV in close pursuit; then, surprisingly, the driver nodded his head in salute, but to whom? Sam wondered. To him . . . or to Hark Bittersweet?

"Bailey," Sam said, "Ridge told me truth is stranger than fiction, and he was right on target, but if we die, we die."

"My own family," Bailey said, "in a conspiracy." She had never felt such shame.

Sam took a corner too fast and almost lost control of the sedan. "I love you, baby."

Bailey threw her shoulders against the back of

the seat, her feet jammed even harder against the floor. Her voice was husky. "I love you too."

Sam had never felt such anger. Taking advantage of Hark Bittersweet's near-fatal skid, he pulled to a stop on the edge of the cliff. "Bailey," he said, "get out. Run."

She almost slapped him for suggesting she do such a thing. How could she leave him? How? "I'm not going anywhere without you!"

He reached over her, flung the door open, and shoved her to the dirt. "Run!" he yelled so loud, he made her ears ring. "Now!"

She did run, and as soon as she cleared the passenger door completely, Sam sped away, the passenger door still open. "Sam!" she screamed. "Sam!"

He never even honked good-bye.

The sports car had righted itself, and Bailey could hear it speeding to catch up with Sam. "We're supposed to stay together," she whispered. "Together!"

But of course she knew what her husband was doing—hero that he was, he was trying to lure Hark Bittersweet and his nameless henchman away from her; he was trying to save her at the risk of losing his own life.

For all Bailey knew, the bearded wild man in the SUV could have been a convict who owed Hark Bittersweet a favor or he could have been a dirty cop for hire. Regardless, this terrible race through the mountains was no dream, not even a nightmare, because in a nightmare, she would be able to wake herself up, and, irrationally, Bailey feared that at the rate things were going, she would never get her chance to see Italy.

Like a broken-down china doll with staring brown eyes, she watched in horror as her goldengirl life slid away into nothingness. She might as well have plunged off the cliff for all the damage Sam had done by leaving her alone.

Alone. How dare he break them apart and leave her? The word *think* and the phrase *get away* became a mantra in Bailey's panic-seized mind: *think-getawaythinkgetaway.*

There were no cops to save the day, and her brave but brutal knight had sped off in his smooth-running engine of steel, and so there was nobody, period. Bailey had to save herself. First, she had to *think*. Next, she had to *get away.*

Even though it was not in her heart just then to thank Sam for protecting her the best way he could under the circumstances, she did have a strong survival instinct, and she did believe in miracles, those redeeming acts of grace that broke down the laws of nature to turn nonbelievers into those who did believe—with all their minds, with all their hopes, and all their dreams: Bailey dreamed of safety.

Once the Trans Am screamed down the highway after Sam, she ran across the open road and into trees. *Think,* said her mind, *get away.*

Bailey ran without looking back. She cut through trees. She fell over slight rises in the earth, then fell inside its many pits and holes. In her panic, she imagined she heard creatures slither between the trees and the tangled brush.

She felt thigh-high weeds bump against her body, their protective thorns tearing at her clothes, their needle-sharp tips ripping tiny holes in her pretty brown flesh. She fell so many times she started to stagger, but on she ran, then on she ran some more.

Pain jarred her body with every step. With the

pain came panic—*think*. This stretch of hillside was home to the super rich. She had to go up, up to safety, up to one of the private roads that weaved through the mountains. She had to get to people, had to get to a phone. She had to . . . *get away*.

Fear for Sam made her heart jump from her chest, then jump from her chest to her throat. The rush of blood pounding through the vessels in her ears deafened every other sound except the rhythm of her own body fluids. Her fluids converged and pumped in a rhythm that sped faster and faster, the liquids pushed through muscle and bone by the primal force of an acute adrenaline high.

She saw the world in slow motion because she herself was the world. As she ran for her life, no one except herself existed, not the deer who roamed the hillside nor the cougar and boar and vermin and whatever else shared the same territory she did just then—*thinkgetawaythink*.

She needed a new plan, a plan that came to her bit by agonizing bit, the jagged fragments of it mixing, then matching to make her bold. The bold feeling transformed her fear into cold, calculated, and critical thinking.

If she screamed, she doubted she would be heard. If she kept running at a reckless, breakneck pace, she might twist an ankle or hurt herself in some other way. She staggered to a stop and collapsed beneath a tree.

She landed on the ground with a thump, looked up, and changed her mind. She stood. In her line of vision was a branch, a lifeline. The branch stretched in a near flat line to the left of the tree: east. East was home to New Hope, but she was a long, long way from ever getting there.

Think.

She jumped once, then again until her arms caught the lowest limb of the tree. She hauled herself up, one leg at a time. She climbed three branches to the sky because three was her lucky number.

As soon as she stilled, she heard noises—slithering noises, rustling noises, scary noises, but for all her cold, careful, and practical thinking, she had salty tears in her eyes. She wiped away the tears with dirty fingers that left grit in their wake. She blinked away the grit, the act creating more tears.

Thinkgetawaythinkgetaway.

The mantra soothed her. The salt water cleared her eyes at about the same time the chant cleared her mind as valiantly, heroically, she pushed her fear to the side. Bailey climbed down from the tree, determined to make it back to the road that brought her up the hillside; at the rate she had been running she was bound to get lost in the cold and in the dark. No more running, she vowed, no more, because as Sam had so accurately said, if it was time to die, it was time to die, and if that was true, so be it.

Bailey walked quickly back down to the road and was careful to stay in the thick patches of undergrowth or near clusters of bushes when she could. She was surprised at how far she had traveled and at how easy it had been to lose her bearings.

The going was rough, and now that her mind was more in control than her emotion-charged high, she sadly discovered she was also wobbly and fatigued. She practiced no formal exercise regimen and so she suffered from the effects of a background limited in aerobic exercise. If she survived, she planned to take up running.

Bailey stubbed her bare sandal-clad toes on small, jagged rocks. The acorns from wild oak trees crunched beneath the soles of her feet, each crunch causing her to hold her breath as she listened for sounds of pursuit by her enemy or rescue by her hero.

Instead of being brown and short and dry, the natural growth in the area was green from the rain and from the mists of low-slung clouds. The terrain was not dense like a forest, nor was it bare like a mountain. The terrain was ripe with crevices, small clusters of rocks, small mounds of dirt and tufts of flowering weeds. It was beautiful. Had she been hiking for pleasure, she would have appreciated that beauty.

Her life was twilight and getting darker. She walked ten minutes among the tall grass, then stopped long enough to get her bearings. Instead of standing, she sat on the ground beneath a young redwood tree. Resting her aching body, she took six cleansing breaths.

At the start of the seventh breath she noticed a crawling sensation. Ants. Not wanting to give away her location, she suppressed the urge to squeal. She doubted she had the energy to run if Hark Bittersweet spotted her.

Getting up slowly, she moved away from the random itching of the ants and from the shelter of the redwood. She felt stuck. Above her, the hillside was an endless series of steps she was too tired to take. Below her, lay possible violence . . . and Sam, always Sam, forever Sam. *I love you. Please . . . be safe.*

She knew the hillside had a beginning and an

end and that one way or another she would be
found. People lived in these hills. Hikers climbed
their peaks. The road running through the hills
was her best chance for help and her potential
killer's best chance to capture her. She could sit
and wait until it was fully dark but then she would
be at the mercy of the elements.

Bailey was falling apart, and she knew it, yes, she
knew it, and she was trying so desperately hard to
hold herself together. Her clear thinking skills were
ebbing away, they were leaving her mind jittery, as
the loss of adrenaline had left her legs jittery, and,
in the absence of clear thought and a willing body,
stark fear once again took center stage. Her life was
a drama and the drama was about to end.

Bailey felt so cold, so horribly disillusioned and
alone. The cold sank into her bones and shook
them until her teeth rattled. She had no jacket.
Her clothes were torn. Her purse, with all her
identification, was in Sam's sedan.

If she wound up dead and eventually found, it
was possible she would remain unidentified, and
there she was, a newly made millionaire, heiress to
a fortune that would return to the very hands Fred
Durham had despised.

Sam . . . Fern . . . Sage . . . I love you.

Meanwhile, Sam was scared spitless for Bailey.
Fear made him reckless, and being reckless made
him bold in his search for her. He honked his
horn again and again and again as he careened
back to the road where he had dumped her: Hark
Bittersweet and his accomplice had finally sped
away, leaving Sam free to backtrack for Bailey—if
only he could find her, if only . . . he could tell

her one last time how sorry he was for leaving her, how very much he loved her.

Sam honked the horn again. He stopped the car, got out, cupped his hands around his mouth to yell, "Bailey! Bailey!"

From her hiding place, Bailey cocked her head to one side and listened hard, harder than she had ever listened in her life.

"Bailey!" the voice screamed. "Bailey!"

Sam, dear God, it's Sam.

Warm tears of relief flowed from Bailey's eyes. "Here!" she said, "I'm here!" He was too far away to hear her, but that did not stop her from being thankful for the miracle she had been given, the miracle of his life being spared a very violent, very painful death.

But she was dead wrong about Sam, he did hear her cry, his soul mate, the other half that made him whole. "Bailey!" In that one word was grief and happiness, joy and pain: relief.

Running full speed, her tangled hair flying, Bailey screamed directions to her hero. "I'm here! Here!"

Sam sprinted toward the sound of her voice in a burst of savage, fighting energy, he sprinted as if tomorrow might never come. He rushed to where she stood, on the point of collapse, and then, miraculously, he had her gripped tight in his hard, muscular arms, had them wrapped around her deliciously sweet and precious body.

Grateful to God for his second chance, Sam slammed a kiss against the warmth of Bailey's mouth, the plump feel of her lips sacred to him, her breath a treasured gift of life, because, without her, the sun would never shine for him again.

Carefully, methodically, Sam rolled his intense

black eyes over the tear-streaked and frightened face of the woman he adored, the shadowed side of his mind consumed with murderous thoughts of violence and revenge.

Gently, protectively, Sam cupped Bailey's cheeks inside the brace of his hands, hands he longed to use to destroy Hark Bittersweet. In a raspy, Bruce Willis *Die Hard* voice he said, "When I find that lying bastard, baby, I'm gonna kill him."

For three full seconds Bailey burned in the fire of her husband's bitter gaze, her near hysterical mind shocked by the rage she confronted. The twin fires of hate and of vengeance blazed away in her hero's eyes, fires hotter than any sun, flames higher than any mountain.

The twin fires of pure malice were born in a ruthless, single-minded passion that had its match in Hark Bittersweet, the first person to notice and comment that Sam indeed had a switch turned off. Sam, who, from the beginning, had never trusted the detective, had only visited the detective at his home when he felt pushed to the wall.

Within those three revealing seconds, Bailey knew she loved Sam, loved him with all her frightened heart and her scattered mind, but had he crossed some line where her love could not reach him? Had he become the very kind of man he despised?

What would happen to herself and to her daughters, Bailey wondered, if Sam acted out on his repressed aggression, all the pent-up anger he felt over the shenanigans at the Painted Lady and the run-in with the crooked law on Highway One?

What would happen if he committed some unspeakable crime in retaliation for Hark Bittersweet's use and abuse of their trust? Sam was dealing with his injured male pride, and logic had nothing to do with pride. It had to do with common sense, for which he was currently in short supply. Gone was her rational Sam, and in his place was an embittered, embattled man.

For once, Bailey's trust was shaken. Never would she have imagined he would kick her to the curb, even if he thought he was doing it for her own safety. Never would she have doubted his self-control when it came to choosing peaceful resistance over violence, never, and yet, there he stood, a raging bull with the red flag of Bittersweet's deceit before him, and a wary wife clasped tight in his powerful arms.

Sam rolled his eyes all over Bailey's face and body, his mind noting the fresh bruises, his soul sensing the emotional pain. The husband in him kicked in, and when it did, so too came the memory of their many years together, not just as man and wife, but as the very best of friends.

Within the boundaries of that union was a faith in American law and its order. It was this faith that helped Sam focus on the good he should do, not the bad he wanted to do. He seriously wanted to wring Hark Bittersweet's neck, but not at the expense of his family or his salvation.

In the end, after they had spoken to the California Highway Patrol about their encounter, Sam and Bailey drove home, to New Hope, back to the place that centered them as a couple, and ultimately as a family. The rest of their vacation would be spent at home, in the sanctuary and haven they had built together, one for the other, a home they shared with the children they had made . . . together.

EPILOGUE

Saturday, one week later
New Hope, California

Morning dawned and as daylight spread across the sky, erasing the night and all its hidden secrets, Bailey felt the healing light of rejuvenation that every new day delivered into her life. It signaled an addition to her store of life experience, a fresh set of opportunities to make whatever was wrong in her life as right as she possibly could make it.

In the morning, her enthusiasm for all things natural and good was set into proper perspective: Dew on the velvety green leaves of the roses in her garden, jays playing with one another on the lawn, hummingbirds finding their way to the red nectar she kept in a feeder on a thick purple ribbon near the kitchen window. For Bailey, life was not about chasing what she wanted, it was about dealing with what she had. She and Sam had a lot.

The house was quiet, Sam and the girls sleeping late. It was the time of day Bailey most enjoyed, and she used the brief moment of personal solitude as a meditation. She was a woman who thoroughly enjoyed her home, the belongings she used to adorn its floors, walls, and windows important, not because they were fancy or expensive, but because they were uniquely her.

In Bailey's home, bargain reproductions of afrocentric prints shared wall space with limited-edition art by Annie Lee and Brenda Joysmith. There was an assortment of nifty flea market finds mixed companionably with treasure gleaned from upscale antique malls, but it was the kitchen that drew her over and over, while reading the paper over coffee, while doing homework with the girls or catching up on daily events with her husband, while snapping beans for dinner, or just plain gabbing on the phone with one of her girlfriends.

Dressed in soft, faded Levi's and a salmon-colored tank top, Bailey opened the pink blinds at the windows in the breakfast nook. The air outside was still, the sky cloud free and the most beautiful shade of blue Bailey had seen in a very long time, beautiful because she was in her own home again, at 1899 Laurel Lane.

In deep appreciation, she admired the distant hills, a peaceful sight that reinforced her sense that she was doing the right thing by closing her catering business to run the Fred Durham Foundation full-time.

She would always cook for her family and friends, but by devoting herself to the foundation, Bailey reenergized her own sense of self-worth. The foundation would move her firmly into the public eye, into a mostly black community that would relish an influx of philanthropic dollars, Durham dollars: Fred would be proud.

Closing her eyes, Bailey deepened her meditation, her inner contemplation of the good things in her personal life. She saw the ferns growing in the shade of twenty-foot flowering trees, she recalled the scent of the cinnamon ferns, her favorites of the many varieties Sam had planted when their oldest daughter, Fern, was born.

In her mind, Bailey walked slowly to the rain-washed and sun-worn wooden bench that nestled near one of several miniature waterfalls Sam had built into their half-acre lot. In her mind, Bailey was whole, safe, happy, and free.

Behind her, Sam entered the kitchen. Without a word, he eased behind her womanly body to loop his arms around the waist that had carried two lovely daughters. More enamored of his wife now than he had been during the year of their first wedding anniversary, Sam buried his nose in her hair, its wiry texture scented like the red roses she favored on the south side of the home they cherished together.

With a soft sigh of satisfaction, Bailey turned in her husband's arms, her face lifted to his humbled gaze. It was she who stood by him as he sorted through and made sense of the violence he came close to committing against Hark Bittersweet.

Had Sam been able to successfully counter the detective's attack by gunfire, he might, this very instant, be in jail himself. As it was, neither man was behind bars. The detective had abandoned his home and San Francisco stomping grounds for parts unknown to the police, who hunted him with a vengeance. Sam was glad: He would rather his hands grip Bailey's hips than grip the bars of a cold and lonely cell in a county jail.

With his eyes, Sam consumed her. At five feet five inches tall, she was soft and lush in all the right places. Her deep ocher-colored eyes were wide and welcoming, her lashes a little wild and scattered, but dark and silky like her brows, to his gentle touch.

Her nose, slightly pointed, her lips, full and well-shaped, were in pleasing proportion on a face that was oblong and cocoa colored. Sam vowed to take nothing for granted about her ever again, not the reddish brown hair on her head to the tangerine polish she favored on her toes.

In turn, Bailey returned his visual seduction. Muscles filled his six-foot frame to perfection, and thanks to regular workouts in a nearby gym, his stomach was fit and phat. His jet-black eyes were all-seeing as they peered into the silky, satin walls of her eternal soul. His nose was wide and afro-classic, as were his strong, dark, truly kissable lips.

When he opened his mouth to speak, she shushed him with a fingertip. Each held the other, chest to chest, hip to hip, thigh to thigh, and outside, as the rising sun dried away the dew from the velvety leaves in Bailey's garden, something unwanted was left for them to find, there, beneath a red river rock on the first step to the Walkers' front door.

It was a note, written on plain white paper. The note said:

"I never meant to kill you or Sam. I was angry and wanted to scare you. I hired a crack junkie to scare you on the road. I took shots at you with my gun, but none of them were aimed at you specifically, just your car. I hit the rear passenger-side three times, never the windows or near the front seats.

Other than the junkie who owed me a favor from my vice-squad days, I'm in this thing by myself. I have no accomplice. Everything done after you left the Painted Lady for the coastline was up to me, so Phoebe killed Sybil, that's true, and no, Bailey, there was no

*conspiracy, just an oddball collection of screwed-up
people, myself included.*

*Everything we did together was true, including the
pursuit of the truth about Fred's death, but the day I
retired, I realized the new life I had planned was over
before it had even got started. You see, I was angry
about the gardens, the botanical gardens near my
home on Dark Hill. Fred left no money for their upkeep
and continuation.*

*People thought I cared about charities for children.
I didn't. Children's charities were Fred's thing, mine
was the botanical gardens. It takes four grand a
month just to pay the utilities and there were countless
other issues at stake regarding the garden's upkeep,
but the final insult was that land developers wanted
to use the site to build yet another condominium com-
plex, as if the city needed another.*

*I had planned to retire and work at the gardens
but without Fred's backing there would have been no
place for me to work. It takes years to build such a
garden, even a small one worthy of showing to the
public, and I hated Fred for that.*

*Like my first wife, a woman I trusted, Fred had
betrayed my friendship on a very elemental level. In
doing so, he became my foe instead of my friend. By
committing suicide the way he did, with a blow-dryer,
he assured himself that you would dig into the crime,
that you wouldn't take what happened to him as an
unfortunate accident.*

*The blow-dryer was his insurance that you would
be involved, his way of thinking much like Sybil's
strategy when she penned Bailey's name on her bedroom wall in blood. All the killing and attempted killing going on was about frustration. Different levels
of it.*

Without Fred's money I'm forced to start a life from

scratch again, and I didn't want to do that. Like a spoiled child, I acted out my fantasy of revenge by attacking the two of you. But being an officer of the law for most of my life, I am pleased to say that my "switch" hasn't been turned off. I don't have the stomach to kill cold-bloodedly. Besides, if you were dead, I'd still be stuck thinking up a new career.

I watched you and your family from a distance this week and even considered doing some harm to your girls, but I'm not that kind of man, not really. If I harmed your family, Sam would do what police everywhere are unable to do, which is find me.

I'm a cop and like I told you before, I'm good at what I do. You Durhams were always in to books and often quoted them. It's a quirk I marveled at, that and your eyes, your nosy natures, and your general indifference toward each other.

I like movies. In Silence of the Lambs, Hannibal Lechter escapes his prison, his boring, predetermined fate and goes on a great adventure. I, too, have escaped boredom and like you, I'm in my own little world, enjoying the good life.

Cheers,

HB

Uncle Fred's Favorite Cake Recipe

Chocolate Delight

- 1 box of fudge cake mix
- 1 box of instant fudge pudding
- 2 tablespoons cocoa
- 5 eggs
- 1/2 cup water
- 1/2 cup oil
- 1/2 teaspoon vanilla
- 1 cup sour cream
- 1/3 bag of chocolate chips
  chocolate syrup

Oil and flour cake pan. Combine dry ingredients in a large bowl. Add liquids. Mix well. Stir in sour cream and chocolate chips. Bake at 350 degrees for fifty minutes or until done. Cool cake on wire rack. Drizzle chocolate syrup over warm cake. Great with vanilla bean ice cream.

Dear Readers:

SACRED LOVE is the fifth book I've published with Arabesque, and as always, I continue to welcome your letters. So far I've heard it all, from fans who enjoy the stories I've written to fans who like some stories but not all. Each book is a journey for me. On each journey, I stretch my writing skills a little farther, my goal being to get stronger and better with each finished book. While I don't write about my personal life, I do write about the things I most enjoy, like cooking and gardening. I hope that over the years as I continue to craft stories, you will continue to tell me how you feel about them. Please send a self-addressed, stamped envelope to my attention and I will write you back. I can be reached at P.O. Box 253, Guthrie, OK 73044. I am currently at work on a new story called SIMPLY MARVELOUS. It should be in stores February 2002.

Sincerely yours,
Shelby Lewis

ABOUT THE AUTHOR

Shelby Lewis lives in Guthrie, Oklahoma, with her husband, Steve, and their teenage sons, Steven and Randal. Her family lives in a cottage-styled house made of brick in a neighborhood bordered by country roads. She has three rowdy dogs named Kasey, Dino, and Tuffy who keep her busy when she isn't writing or working in her husband's coffee shop. She enjoys gardening, spending time with her friends, and relaxing by the fire with a good book.

BOOK YOUR PLACE ON OUR WEBSITE AND MAKE THE ARABESQUE ROMANCE CONNECTION!

We've created a customized website just for our very special Arabesque readers, where you can get the inside scoop on everything that's going on with Arabesque romance novels.

When you come online, you'll have the exciting opportunity to:

- View covers of upcoming books

- Learn about our future publishing schedule (listed by publication month and author)

- Find out when your favorite authors will be visiting a city near you

- Search for and order backlist books

- Check out author bios and background information

- Send e-mail to your favorite authors

- Join us in weekly chats with authors, readers and other guests

- Get writing guidelines

- AND MUCH MORE!

Visit our website at
http://www.arabesquebooks.com

More Sizzling Romance From
Brenda Jackson